The Other Side Of Carrie Cornish

by

Kate Jay-R

Copyright 2018 Kate Jay-R

Cover Design adapted from Royalty Free Image at
www.shuttersock.com

All characters are fictional, and any resemblance to anyone living or dead is accidental

Acknowledgements

To all those family and friends who've been a support to me, a heartfelt thanks. To everyone who's suffered with neighbour noise, this is for you. To my fellow camapigners, online and out there, fighting the injustices of the welfare system and years of austerity, this is for you.

January 2013

The woman's family and loved ones have heard the local news bulletin with its routine phrasing. Critically ill in hospital after a violent argument with a neighbour. Rushed to hospital, having sustained a head injury. A neighbour is helping police with their enquiries. But for her family and loved ones, there is nothing standard about it. The clipped expressions, devoid of emotion, make it sound so much like someone else, not the woman they know and love. It leaves them feeling disoriented and a bit unreal. Even so, they wait and pray, even those that don't believe in prayer. If only they'd known. They did know, didn't they? But they didn't know it would crossover into something life-threatening. Just how do you know the moment? This sort of thing doesn't happen in nice towns, even nice towns with seedy corners...

Twelve months earlier

Day One

They say the way I see things is a bit hinky. Like when you take a picture and it needs straightening in iPhoto. Only it's my mind that wants tweaking and you need a shrink to do that. I thought I would preface this with that information, Mr Vowells, as you've asked us to keep a diary for a month.

I don't know how to begin or what sort of information you want from us, Mr Vowells, but you need to know that Sandy has MS and I have what they call Mental Health issues as follows: Generalised Anxiety, Panic Disorder, OCD, Social Phobia and some Agoraphobia. But Sandy and I are both articulate and responsible people who just want a quiet life. Sandy is in his early sixties and though I'm fifteen years younger, I've reached an age where I want the same too.

We chose to live somewhere quiet. The Torquay estate where we moved from was so rough that even the dogs were on an ASBO. That's what me and Sandy used to joke about, although it wasn't really funny. Not when you're in the thick of it. Though when we first moved there we were probably the neighbours from hell with our loud music. But you reach a time in your lives, I suppose. You reach a point where you outgrow noise. Where you crave quiet. So we came here to this part of South Devon to get away from that kind of life. OK, it's not proper country here, not like where my parents live. Where the air is filled with the sound of clip-clopping horses and tractors, and you'll find sheep and cows and even alpacas in the fields, bred for their wool which fetch a nice price, not so much for the alpaca farmers but at the ready-made clothes' end of the market. We didn't want to be *that* rural, Sandy and I, but nothing too urban either. So we chose this small market town on the River Dart for its individual shops with hand-crafted knick knacks and none of your whopping megastores—they'd just make me giddy. We chose this town for its creative appeal and applied to live here.

We heard about some shared ownership houses being built through Shires Housing Association and we applied for our house here at Pennycott, before it was even built. We saw the architect's drawings, beautiful white houses in a neoclassical style. Some with two bedrooms, some with three. The sizes of the rooms looked reasonable, and the two bedroomed houses had longer galley kitchens than we were used to. We had just enough money for a fifty per cent share between us, and we saw the land where our house was to be built. We travelled back and forth to watch its progress, we saw the breeze blocks going up, and then slowly a row of two and three bedroom houses began to take shape, cement mixers cluttering the site.

Later, when the insides of the Pennycott houses were almost complete, we came down to visit the house we'd reserved. There was a Portakabin and a site manager and a lot of smart sales people wandering about in the rain. There were no gardens, yet. Just concrete mixers and plenty of sloppy pink Devon mud. Without gardens the houses seemed so close together. Only a few footsteps from Number 3 (ours) to Number 1(two doors up). But space, like time, seems further away when it's packed with lots of detail: fences and plants and sheds. And our walls grew—once we'd moved in—while the other walls around us shifted away.

Until the Tragos.

That's our main news headline. I'm mentioning the news because it is important to people like Sandy and me who spend a lot of time at home. Sometimes it's our only form of escape.

*

Carrie sits back and surveys her handiwork. She decides that Day One, Day Two, Day Three etc will read better than penning in the actual date. That way, if she doesn't fill it out every day—if there are gaps, say, on quieter days—Mr Vowells, the Environmental Health Officer will be none the wiser and it will read as a continuous document.

'They've gone out, Carrie.' Sandy's shoulders relax as he announces what should be cause for celebration. But she and Sandy are all wound up waiting for the Tragos return. They've got to the stage where they can't enjoy the quiet. Carrie notes this down in pencil in the journal. Then removes her earplugs.

'Sand? Read what I've put so far.'

Having given it the once over Sandy shakes his head. Don't mention being hinky or your mental health issues, he advises: there's still this stigma and they might dismiss the rest of what you say. She could just write health problems. He wouldn't mention about the estate where they lived before. Not relevant, he says. More is less. Cut all the mention of our house being built. Cut the mention of getting giddy in the megastores: it makes *you* sound like the one with problems. I know you've had your issues, Carrie, but it's not relevant here. Make *them* your focus. Cut to the quick.

She'll have to start again with a new Day One. She'll begin it tomorrow. Or on a very bad day. Not that she wants there to be very bad days, but it's a form of refuge, having somewhere to vent your spleen. She was doing so well up until recently—even returning to work at the

Blue Cross charity shop two mornings a week—until the Tragos.

But this lunchtime all she wants is to make the most of the quiet because the Tragos have gone out. Probably to Trago Mills, Sandy suggests hopefully, Trago Mills being, as everyone in the South West knows, a big superstore-cum-theme-park whose fairytale turrets you can see from the motorway just outside Newton Abbot. Carrie has heard there are two more of them in Cornwall. She and Sandy once heard their neighbours in Number 4 mention a trip to Trago Mills which is how they acquired their name. But the Tragos hardly ever go out and when they do it's for frustratingly short periods, which rather rules out Trago Mills because no sooner has their car roared out of the car park than it roars back again. Probably lack of funds, Carrie notes, judging by the overheard rows on the matter, through the walls or spilling from the back door. If only the kids could run around in the park—even the themed park at Trago Mills—or take a hike in the country, she's sure their cabin fever would soon disperse. But it's only February, spring still a way off. Maybe they will go out more once the weather improves.

It's a rare treat these days to hear as well as see the end of the news. Nowadays, they often have to tape it and then whizz-watch it at some later time. Whizz-watching is what you do when you're tired or when your head can't take much more than headlines. You fast-forward on your remote, stopping at bits that look interesting. Carrie hates to whizz through the foreign news, and all the momentous occurrences in the Middle East but she can't keep up with it. She reflects on how they've shared this news interest—she and Sandy—since they met in the nineties. His was a more serious interest. He always knew what was going on in the wider world. She felt hers was perhaps more frivolous as she watched the flowers, the crowds, the tears, the book signings, the procession after Diana's death. She watched the funeral and bought *Candle In The Wind.* Sandy scowled and said there were loads of other news stories not getting covered but the princess's death made Carrie forget her own problems.

But then came 9/11 and Saddam Hussein and WMD. News was no longer about royal liaisons and tragedies, if it ever had been, and she became more savvy. She knew then that Saddam was bluffing—that's what you do when you want to be counted in with the big boys. You play a game. I've got weapons in my pocket, you say.

*

Day One

I shall begin the diary for real today because the Tragos have returned from some short break. I can't believe they were away for a few days but Sandy and I really noticed the hush. You'd think the last few days would have been bliss because we could hear the quiet next door for the first time in weeks—since the Tragos moved in, in fact—but we were just waiting for the storm to return.

We did get a brief glimpse of how life used to be when the Zamoras lived there, though it was the Zamoras—being a young, professional couple—who bought the other fifty per cent share of their house from Shires Housing Association, and so became home owners. Once owner-occupiers, they were free to sell their house to whom they pleased when they were ready to move. And they sold it to the council. We only found this out afterwards, Sandy and I. We couldn't work it out at first, and I don't wish to sound judgemental, but the

Tragos didn't look like home owners. We thought maybe they were renting from the Zamoras until, after a bit of delving and discreet enquiries, we discovered that the Zamoras had sold their house to the council. Our worst fears confirmed. We're not snobs, me and Sandy, really we're not. Ask anybody. I was born on the outskirts of Liverpool and spent my formative years in very thrifty circumstances, like many of my generation, and we've lived among nice people on council estates, but you can tell just by looking at the Tragos the kind of people they are. Sandy says they are chavs, even though I hate that word. But you can imagining them sitting around in the evenings, their eyes glued to reality TV. They are like some of the people from our last home on the Torquay estate who were described as milking the state to fund their tattoos and bling. We came here to put all that nasty stuff behind us. Not just those people, but the people who said nasty things of those people.

The Tragos moved into Number 4 next door in January. At first I thought they had just the one child. But there was something about the way Little Un was cycling round and round on those flagstones on his own. 'Gerrout the way,' he ordered of all obstacles in his path. And him no more than three. I thought then, I thought he's being primed for hooliganism, you can see it in his shaved head, in the pretend tattoo on his arm, in the way he's kicking at his red and yellow plastic petrol pump. And you should have heard the accent on him. I could barely understand what he was saying. I like accents, really I do—(they tell me I have a gentle Crosby sing-song)—but not on tiny kids. Not thick accents. It sounds precocious. Sinister even. Accents shouldn't kick in until later and then only gently and gradually. But playing there on his own, Little Un didn't look like the centre of his parents' world. Where were they? They hardly noticed he was there. Odd for a first child, I thought.

I watched from the vantage point of our upstairs back bedroom when his mum and dad first arrived and unloaded their van. His dad looked like a Pit Bull. Stocky. Wide flat face. Slitted eyes. Mouth snarling upwards. All he needed was a chain round his neck. I'm not one to judge, ask anyone who knows me, but I have a Pit Bull phobia, so anyone who resembles one in any shape or form scares the shit out of me. You don't mess with that kind of face. Little Un, he has the same kind of features. The woman, the mother, well, she looks really hard. Dyed burgundy hair. I've got nothing against dyed hair—I tone mine. Honey. I like it. Sandy likes it. But hers looks brittle and brutal. And she has tattoos. Like the Trago man. He has a barcode tattooed on the back of his neck. I mean—what the fuck? Hers is a Celtic tattoo so she's not all bad, though when she last wore short sleeves (yes, in winter) it looked less Celtic and more barbed wire. And she has these thongs showing above the waistband of her jeans. They're all twisted, not an erotic sight. You'd have to seriously downsize your thighs to carry it off. You have to be skinny and twenty, and skinny and twenty she ain't. She probably wears them round the house while eating her cornflakes and bringing in the milk. Thongs are not sexy in this context, let me tell you. I got this sinking feeling. Like I knew something was wrong. Watch out for that rising or sinking feeling, Trisha says at the Anxiety Group.

It's not the kid's fault. We could hear the terrier dad carping at the toddler from the off. After a few days we thought—me and Sandy—we thought, OK. So they're not Family of the Year but as long as they don't bother us we can live and let live. We've lived among all sorts on the housing estate where we used to live.

But then one night I could hear her talking on her

mobile outside. I wasn't earwigging. I just couldn't help over-hearing. 'Getting my boys back tomorrow,' she said and my body went rigid. Not boy, she'd said *boys*. That had to be at least two, on top of Little Un already in situ.

Turned out to be three. Ages ranging from five to ten or thereabouts. All with accents. Well, these boys arrived with a bang, a crash and a thump as boys will. They were leaping about the house and up and down the stairs, and round your lady's chamber. All the time shouting and yelling. OK, we thought, Sandy and I. They've just got a new house, they're bound to be a bit excited, they'll calm down soon. We're reasonable, compassionate people, even though we suffer with poor health. But this noise went on and on. That's when we realized we should have nipped it in the bud straight away instead of being so damned reasonable. I suppose some people have an art for spotting a softie. A mug. Someone they can take advantage of. A natural gift you might say. I wonder how they do it and how it is we let them?

But enough is enough, Mr Vowells.
Sandy likes to read quietly or listen to Radio 3 or 4, but even when we turned the radio up we could still hear their noise. It was like an earthquake. I started pacing and begging Sandy to go round there and say something. He knows how anxious I get in situations like this but Sandy said it'd look better coming from a woman. 'If the man answers he might think I'm picking a fight,' he said. 'A man like that won't hear the reason in my voice.'

'Hullo? So it's OK if he makes purée of me?' I had a picture of the Trago man, arms folded like a bull bar across his four-by-four chest as he answered the door.

'I'll come with you,' Sandy said. 'Then we can show a united front.'

I was so angry about the noise that it overtook my anxiety, anyway. I went into 'character' in my head. I pretended I was Seroxat Sid. Not that I'm on Seroxat at the moment but I have been in the past. I should explain at this juncture that Seroxat Sid is my alter-ego in times of difficulty. Once in character, my feet felt firm and resolute and we went round there, me with earplugs in hand. It was the Trago woman who answered, as it happened, a few of her brats in tow (the Trago terrier didn't surface). Never mind him, she looked like she might make purée of the pair of us so we introduced ourselves and said that sometimes we worked from home (which is true in Sandy's case—he does some freelance articles).

'My kids have been cooped up in a B & B and it's just so nice for them to have space to play,' Mrs Trago said, by way of explanation for the noise. 'As a child I wasn't allowed to run up and down the stairs—so I want my kids to be able to.'

'Oh we do understand,' we said.

'But the walls are that thin,' I said. 'Like 20 denier stockings!'

'We hope you can see our point of view,' Sandy added and she promised to keep the noise down. Sandy and I went home feeling lighter and brighter for being assertive and hoping there it would end. We wanted to give her the benefit of the doubt. We are tolerant people, Mr Vowells.

But we were woken by elephants in clodhoppers at 7.30 this morning. We could hear every accompanying yell. 'Shut up, Logan,' one of the kids shouted. We could hear their squeals above the extractor fan in the bathroom and believe me that has a loud motor. Logan—he's the three-year-old. The youngest. They all have these funny names. Not bog-standard boys' names. But surnames as first names. Sandy says that's very chavvy.

Later in the morning I could hear a lot of loud

screaming in their yard. It's Saturday and the kids are home. Other kids go out on a Saturday, but not these. Sandy saw them crash into our fence twice. The whole fence shook he said. He is a patient man but he stood there clenching his fists. 'If the little buggers do it again...' he said. It's their parents, you see. They don't tell them not to. We feel we should go out there and reprimand them but they're not our responsibility. They're unsupervised, you see. It's all well and good politicians talking about respect and responsibility but no-one's teaching these kids to respect their neighbour's property and if they're not told, Logan and his brothers will carry on crashing their vehicles into our fence.

You should see the state of their back garden. It's become a dumping ground for old tat and containers full of oil. The garden used to look cared-for when the Zamoras lived there and although we didn't like the way they concreted over the grass, it would be used as a patio in the summer when the Zamoras did their entertaining. Now the boys have to negotiate their way through this obstacle course, giving them even less space to play in what's an already cramped garden. Sorry, yard. But why should they respect it? Your colleague at the council said they were only temporary—the house has been designated for "temporary families in need of assistance"—those were her words, though when I spoke on the phone to her superior, Mr Hope-Gapp, he said temporary might mean two years. Two years! I can't stand two months of this, let alone two years. But the rest of us at Pennycott have a vested interest in our properties.

As I write there is constant screaming outside and I'm driven to turn my iPod up full. When you came round, Mr Vowells, after our first complaint—which wasn't a complaint as such because we blamed the poor soundproofing—it was a relief when you and your colleague took us seriously and did your own basic tests on the wall (largely knocking) and could hear for yourself how flimsy the structure was, how sounds resonate throughout our whole house. (Forgive me, Mr Vowells, but someone just has to fart next door and all the houses along this row would shake.) But the fact that the noise transmission was demonstrated in front of Mrs Trago was a stroke of genius because she was able to hear it too and your confirmation gave credence to our position so that we didn't look like whingeing neighbours but tolerant people with a genuine grievance. This certainly helped matters and after your first visit things seemed better for a short while. We also felt hopeful at your mention of 'soft furnishings' to help quell 'impact noise' as you called it.

*

Carrie rests her pen and shows her revised Day One to Sandy who tells her to scrub most of it until the bit that says 'we went round there—me with earplugs in hand', substituting neighbours for Tragos, of course, and deleting the word 'brats', because the council will have the rest of the background, he says, although he agrees it is an odd place to begin. He tells her she could start with, after several failed approaches to our neighbours in the past, for example—*insert an example*—we have decided to log our complaints in the form of a journal as suggested by yourself last time we contacted you about the continuing noise. Brilliant, she says. Sandy has a succinct way about him. She tries not to look to him as a father figure but sometimes she can't help herself. She wonders why he doesn't write the diary himself but he says it needs the emotive side—how the two of them *feel* about it. He says he'd approach it from the head and as a result his journal would be clinical and matter-of-fact.

She thinks back to the time when she and Sandy first moved to Pennycott. She can't begin to describe that feeling of owning their own home. She looked around and thought, 'This is mine. All mine. Well...half mine, if you count Sandy's half. Well, quarter mine, really, if you count Shires' half.' She looked on the house as you might a child. The housing association like distant grandparents, only stepping in when they needed to, or when she and Sandy needed them to.

The year was 2001, a world away from now. A lot happened in that year but it was all Foot and Mouth reports at the time they moved away from Torquay. Foot and Mouth filled the local news every day. It was mainly down here in Devon, and up in Cumbria. Healthy animals being slaughtered. The government brought in the army to help. She remembers how she shuddered at all that horrid burning and digging, at the sight of great scoops full of dead sheep flumping out into trenches. Same with the cows being shot, reminding her of Belsen. It was all about money, of course. Farm animals—such a peaceful, exploited lot—were a commodity. People felt sorry for the farmers, but Carrie couldn't stomach all this open-air slaughter. By early April the cases of Foot and Mouth had reached one thousand. They gave a running total every day and she and Sandy listened as the numbers rose day on day, Devon being one of the worst places affected. Farmers were losing their livelihoods, animals their lives, tourism its trade, hotels their custom. Dartmoor was closed, grids were disinfected. By the end of April over two million animals had been slaughtered. Two million! And Carrie remembers looking at her cup of tea. Or, more precisely, she looked at the painted pictures of sheep on her cup who could boast a nice life with their fluffy bodies, like clouds, leaping across the sky. They had a naïve optimism, those ceramic sheep.

There is always something grounding—if not groundbreaking—about the news. Now, more than a decade on, the news is even more depressing, at home as well as globally. The politics of austerity have taken over from the good times, and the government are gunning for the disabled and chronically ill; for people like her and Sandy.

Sandy returns from a short sojourn to the communal bins with some local neighbourhood news. 'I've just spoken to the new neighbours in Number 5. Well, mainly to him. The name's Rick O'nions.'

Carrie looks at him questioningly.

'Spelt like onions, but he insisted it's as if there's an apostrophe, as in O'Hara.'

Carrie has seen these neighbours fleetingly: a thirty-something couple who seem to take a natural pride in their new home and neighbourhood and have the appearance of being pleasant and quiet—if the hush from that direction is anything to go by—although Sandy and Carrie would be hard pushed to hear anything above the Tragos.

'Anyway, I told them they were welcome to use our parking space for their second car as we don't have one at present,' Sandy adds. 'Even if it is one of those horrid four-by-four SUV gas guzzlers.' Carrie adjudges this to be a smart move. It not only gets them in their new neighbours' good books, it also shows that they are good, considerate neighbours themselves.

Carrie hopes that these neighbours might become their allies against the Tragos, although the new neighbours' house and that of the Tragos is separated by a wide flight of steps, thereby offering them some protection and distance from the noise. Carrie hates to have already judged the new young couple to be a respectable working couple. After all, they have already ascertained that Mr Trago has some sort of job that keeps him away from the premises during daytime hours on weekdays, only returning in his dirty white van after 6 o'clock. In some sense this is a relief to Carrie, not having to be a party to his thundering presence or the domestic conflicts between him and Mrs Trago that abound at weekends. On the other hand, Mrs Trago is alone having to contain her brood when he isn't around, and though he bellows at them on his return from work if they aren't doing as he wants them to do, he does seem to have some control over their noise—even if it is an ominous and repressed quiet during the evening hours.

Carrie turns her head and thoughts to the house on their left: Number 2 Pennycott, which seems to have been empty for the last few weeks. They've not seen hide nor hare of Edith, their eccentric elderly neighbour who lives there alone. Edith, a widow, is small and vulnerable and has always cared about her neighbours. She's been there since the beginning—lending this sense of camaraderie among the original residents. They all looked out for each other, back then, and there was this sense of community of sorts. This was something Carrie and Sandy had been searching for. But over the years, as the original residents gradually sold up and new residents moved in, the sense of community has diminished.

Since the Tragos, Carrie and Sandy haven't even been able to keep abreast with the latest developments in Edith's life. They should really find out from Melvyn Styles, the elderly gentleman at Number 1 Pennycott and good friend of Edith's. He might know if she's ever coming back or selling up. Carrie banishes the thought into the back room of her head. She doesn't like the thought of change, the thought of one of the original residents, especially Edith, not being on site any more.

*

Day Two

The news today is that my sleep was disturbed last night from all the worry about the noise and the effect it's having on my nerves. Then, when I did get off to sleep around 6 am, I was brutally woken to more screaming and jumping about, less than two hours later. I felt shattered and on edge. It's a lovely Sunday afternoon in March and the boys haven't gone out *all day*. There's an assortment of balls and frisbees in our garden. I did once return a frisbee to Mrs Trago. It was flamingo-pink with the name Bailey on it—Bailey being the next-to-youngest. 'Is this one of yours?' I said, handing it over the fence. 'Oh yeah, ta,' she said. That's not the only time I returned one of their stray toys either. After the frisbee incident, I did once tell her, as we coincided on the flight of steps up to the car pack at the back, that a Space Hopper had come over our fence and that we'd throw it back over. I mean, how does a Space Hopper get over a fence without considerable effort? They're not lightweight things. Sandy and I don't bother any more. Our garden is festooned with balls of all shapes and colours and weights. They're scattered across our borders and the small patch of grass but if they can't even be arsed collecting them then they don't deserve to have them back. We're not their slaves—we're not here to run around after them. I can't begin to understand it, though. When we were kids we'd politely knock on the door with 'I'm very sorry but my ball's gone in your garden.' I thought they had no money, this family—they don't take the kids out anywhere, that's for sure. But they must have money to burn if they can afford to lose so many balls.

4.35 pm. They've been screaming and tearing about the garden for the last half hour. I yelled 'shut up, shut up' but no-one heard me. No-one *could* have heard me. I went upstairs to see what was going on. You should have heard the language, Mr Vowells. 'Get off my f***ing bike' followed by a horrible high-pitched yell that went on and on. This was the *three*-year-old using this language, I kid you not. I suppose I felt sad to think of this kid losing his innocence at such a young age. It doesn't surprise me, mind, not when I hear the Trago Terrier effing and blinding at them all the time. He roars. I was terrified the first time I heard it. It was like *I* was being yelled at and that put me on edge. I've heard him shout all sorts to the kids. Like 'get in your fucking bed now, Logan!' Mrs Trago yells at them too. She calls them 'you little shits' and stuff like that. It's unsettling. You like to think of your neighbours as peaceful beings getting on with their own lives, but all this stops me leading a peaceful life and I have had problems with my nerves and it's not fair.

As for Macklin, the second oldest boy, he's at that age where freckles are beginning to appear—usually an angelic sight, but there's nothing angelic going on with this kid. All that expectorating. Boy, can he spit for England—he could give some of those premiership footballers a run for their money. This boy is only seven or eight, for pity's sake, but you can already hear the crack in his voice. I was thinking about WMD only recently and now we have our very own weapon of mass destruction next door. The Trago Terrier's penis, for one—all those monsters it has spawned.

I wondered why the parents weren't saying anything when all that was kicking off in the garden. Then we saw their car return and the Trago parents getting out. There was Mr Trago in a black Puma T-shirt and the barcode visible on the back of his neck as he turned to get something from the back; and the trademark partial thong poking above Mrs Trago's waistband and I saw then that the kids had been left *unsupervised*. God knows for how long. One of the kids could have gone out in the road and got run over. In fact, the little one *did* nearly get run over once already, we heard. It was only the quick thinking of the oldest brother that saved him from the jaws of death, so Edith next door said, not long after they first moved in. But if the Tragos don't even care about their kids, why should they give a fiddler's fart about their neighbours?

*

Carrie flops against Sandy.

He's been known by the name Sandy since secondary school on account of his colouring, and also because he much prefers it to his real name: Reginald. He never has been a Reginald. He's a young sixty-two, and though he has heaps of fossilized lines, he's no slap head, his locks defying his age, escaping as they like to do from an occasional peaked hat. He used to be a Radio 1 man who liked his music loud and proud, like she did, when they were in Torquay, though this is going back a bit to another track in their lives. Now he's more your Radio 4 kind of bloke.

It's only 7.40 pm. The pounding footsteps are still wearing them down. They have had to turn the TV up.

'Do you remember that time my ears were blocked, Sand? A couple of years ago?'

'When they needed syringing?'

'Uh-huh. That's how I wish I was now. Deaf. That comes to something, doesn't it? When you'd rather be deaf.'

'Can I see what you've written?'

Carrie hands over her latest journal entry. It is in rough at the moment, ready to be copied in to the neat journal later. He says some of it's fine but to substitute 'bothered' for 'arsed' in the phrase 'if they can't be arsed collecting them'. He says just because they—the Tragos—are fluent in expletives, doesn't mean that she has to stoop to the lowest common denominator. And she can't, just cannot, include the bit about the Trago's phallus. It will discredit the rest. He says there are a couple of other things. Don't mention their money, or lack of. There was something you've written—where is it now?—about them having money to burn. Here it is. You don't want to sound judgemental. It doesn't matter if they're princes or paupers—it's the noise that's the issue, the intrusion on our right to the Quiet Enjoyment of our Home. They've got this phrase from Chris Vowells, the Environmental Health Officer, as well as Shires Housing Association who bandied the term about in the Residents' Charter, a copy of which was hastily stuffed through next door's letter box as soon as the noise problem reared its head. Strictly speaking the Tragos now come under the auspices of the council and not the housing association and are therefore not duty-bound to sign the charter. However, Sandy said the council will have similar requirements outlined in their own tenancy agreement. Recently, she and Sandy wrote to Mr Hope-Gapp, the head of housing at the council, expressing their concerns about the noise.

Eventually they receive a reply from a Liz Fletcher.

Dear Mr and Mrs Cornish

I refer to your letter dated 13th April. My manager has asked me to write to you directly as I manage the temporary accommodation.

I can confirm that this Authority owns No 4 Pennycott. This Council has a number of properties which it owns or leases for use as temporary accommodation. No 4 Pennycott is one of the most recent, which has been purchased and will be used for families in need of assistance.

We have spoken with the tenant with regard to the noise levels, as well, and she says that the noise is not late at night and is just the children playing. She tries to keep the noise levels down for the neighbours benefit and for her own. Your complaint came to us when the children were on their Easter holiday so hopefully with the children back at school, during the day is now quieter. This property will be their 'home' until we can house them permanently with a Housing Association.

Yours sincerely

Liz Fletcher
Housing Resources Officer

'Pffft.' Carrie immediately phones up Ms Fletcher (pressing the phone buttons like she is poking someone's eyes out). When she finally gets Ms Fletcher on the line, Carrie points out that the school holidays account for a large chunk of the year and that they are *not* holidays for Carrie and Sandy. Carrie wonders how it is that Liz Fletcher can just take Mrs Trago's word for it, that it is 'just the children playing'. Carrie wants to scream down the blower at the gullible Ms Fletcher: *hullo? this isn't children just playing.* She invites Ms Fletcher to come and listen for herself, which of course Ms Fletcher is never going to do. Even if Liz Fletcher did come round the Tragos wouldn't at that moment be making a noise.

Carrie calls it the appointment effect: your dodgy back's suddenly fine when you're at the doctor's. Your faulty boiler miraculously works when you call out a man to repair it. As for the bit about the noise not being late at night, that's a bit like saying, Well, you may have been assaulted on the nose but be grateful your mouth is OK.

Carrie then phones Mr Hope-Gapp who is defensive about the council's actions. They've done nothing underhand, he says, and landlords buy up properties all the time. Carrie again wants to know just how temporary is temporary. Mr Hope-Gapp eventually confirms what he has told them before—that it could be eighteen months to two years at which point Carrie yelps 'two *years*?' Mr Hope-Gapp also intimates that the Tragos are quite happy where they are which is all too much for Carrie. 'Happy? *Happy*? What about our fucking happiness?' The fact that she saves this outburst for Sandy rather than Mr Hope-Gapp is rather fortunate since, as Sandy rightly points out, it wouldn't have furthered their cause any. He advises her to keep a lid on it, darling, if she possibly can.

Carrie wonders why all this should be happening to her and Sandy at this time. They don't want to be battling with the authorities—they just want a quiet life. Though, of course, life is rarely quiet. Life is full of news. Local news, world news, coming through their TV sets every day. The news gives back perspective to their lives. If she just focusses on news, old or new, then she's able to keep hold of that perspective.

Carrie remembers back to 2001, the eventful year when they moved to No 3 Pennycott. Wasn't that also the year George Harrison died? The second Beatle to go? She didn't realize until she turned on the TV expecting to see *Ready Steady Cook* and saw George Harrison instead that she knew. She'd had blood in her phlegm that morning for no reason and he died of throat cancer. Her mum has always said she's got a bit of the psychic in her. But being a daughter of Liverpool (if you can call Crosby real Liverpool which the natives don't) that sort of news is important to her. That's not to say it's not important to others, the Beatles being an international phenomena and all, but it's especially important to her.

Carrie returns to the present and thinks about the conversation with Mr Hope-Gapp. She thinks of the name Hope-Gapp: how it couldn't be more apt. She and Sandy have a hope gap in their lives. But a name is not enough for her. She likes to have an image of who she's communicated with. She looks him up on LinkedIn and finds that apart from his plus-sized nose which overshadows the small line of mouth, he is just another late- middle-aged suit. Liz Fletcher, on the other hand, is younger, in a red jacket. She has small-rectangular glasses and pale straight hair. Chris Vowells is the only one who seems approachable and a bit more human. Maybe it's because they met him in person when he came to investigate their concerns. Maybe it was his casual dress, his avuncular gingery beard and tight curly hair.

In a rare quiet interlude, Carrie can't help noticing the absence of Edith to their other side. When the Tragos first moved in she would try escaping to Edith's—her house made Carrie feel peaceful, with its books and vintage furniture and proper cups and saucers. She also thought Edith might have heard the noise too, through two walls. She was sure she must have done but on the other hand Edith is a people pleaser and of that generation that doesn't like to make a fuss. A former schoolmistress and a Buddhist, she is more than a little eccentric and not one with whom you can easily ally yourself when it comes to neighbourhood difficulties. 'In a world of her own' and 'off with the fairies' are expressions that easily sprang to mind where Edith is concerned. If she chooses to pass the time of day chatting, then Edith can keep up with the best of them, though it is more usual for her to blank people, something Carrie used to take personally but now views it as just another Edith idiosyncrasy. Even so, Mrs Trago seemed the least likely candidate for her attention and conversation. But Carrie remembers a conversation she had with Edith after Logan—the youngest of the Trago boys—had apparently gone out into the road and nearly got run over had it not been for the quick reactions of one of his brothers. Edith had spoken to Mrs Trago and had given Logan first aid—he'd injured his wrist—and spoken very highly of Mrs Trago. 'A nicer person you couldn't wish to meet,' she said which had Carrie wondering whether they were at crossed purposes. If Edith saw Mrs Trago this way, Carrie felt she should try too—instead of being judgemental.

She realizes she is trying to keep Edith in the present tense.

'I miss Edith, Sandy. Did Melvyn Styles at Number 1 say any more to you about her?'

'Edith?' Sandy doesn't look up from his laptop, preoccupied as he is with some online campaign. 'Yeah, she's in poor health and is no longer managing in her house.'

'Is that what Melvyn told you?'

'Yeah. A few weeks ago—I did tell you. He said she was in a nursing home and her house is up for sale. Something about wanting to move closer to her daughter up country.'

Maybe Sandy did tell her or maybe he just thought he did. She's sure she would have remembered the bit about the nursing home and Edith's proposed move up country. Either way, Carrie wishes she'd not asked now. Her worst fears realized. 'That'll mean more new neighbours, Sandy. If Edith goes. That'll mean more stress, just wondering who they might be. Waiting for them to settle in and settle down.'

Sandy tells her not to catastrophize. 'Any new neighbours will be part home owners like us. With a vested interest in the property.'

She is comforted by this thought, even though it is terrible of them to be thinking like this: us homeowners versus them council tenants.

*

Days Three & Four

I woke yesterday morning with a potential headache because I was torn from sleep by screaming and shouting kids. This doesn't set you up well for the day, at the best of times, Mr Vowell's, but when you feel a throb in your temples, you should be able to have more quality sleep to prevent it morphing into a full blown migraine.

By four o'clock I was ready to get my head down again, I was just adjusting my pillow, the duvet pulled over me, when there was more screaming and shouting, and doors slamming. I heard someone shouting 'Macklin' repeatedly, and knew the kids were back from school.

'How's your potential headache?' Sandy asked. 'It's real now,' I said, grappling for my painkillers. I could have weeped, but weeping only makes a pounding head worse. I felt grim with the bumps and thumps and bashing and yelling that seemed to go on for hours and oh the pain in my head. It was like I had a raised sore bump with someone twisting a corkscrew down into my skull.

I could hear the parents shouting repeatedly at the kids to go to sleep at 9.25 pm. I registered the time on my clock as Sandy had put the lamp on and brought me a drink. There was still a kid screaming at ten o'clock.

This morning, day four, after a pill fest to dull the pain and knock me out, I woke with a new pain in the form of knots in my stomach, and not any old loose slipknot. Probably a double fisherman's knot, though I'm not as au fait with such things as Sandy, him being male and all. My nerves feel jangled. And I feel like I'm living *inside* a headache.

But I feel the poor house is being assaulted, as well as me. I feel miserable and weepy and unable to enjoy any quality of life. I feel invaded. I can't even go on the phone to my friends, Clo and Sofe, and hear myself talk, because of kids screaming outside the front door. It's affecting the whole of my being. It's almost like, name a part of the body, and I can tell you something wrong with mine. I used to swear by a homeopathic remedy by the name of Kali Phos. arising from a time when I part-completed a homeopathy correspondence course until I got disillusioned with the whole concept of homeopathy and it stopped working for me. Maybe it never did and I was kidding myself. But I'm assaulting myself with 'proper' medication now: Co-codamol, Nurofen Plus, Gaviscon. I need stronger tranquillisers so I can sleep at night. And I need to make an appointment with my GP to get back on Seroxat.

*

Days Five to Ten of Carrie's journal are more like time logs, listing the time and nature of the noise, some days having many more time entries, like the weekends.

Sandy is of the view that this is the way the journal

should be taking shape: with a list of the facts, whereas Carrie finds it soulless. It doesn't fully portray how she's feeling or the rapid destruction that is taking hold internally.

She will go back to her old ways. She's sure when she began the journal Sandy had said she should write it from the heart, rather than the head as he would write it.

*

Day Eleven

It's the spring half-term, what they used to call Whitsun, maybe they still do for all I know. I never used to notice too much when the school holidays were, now I dread them. The kids next door are thumping and jumping and shouting all day long, on and off, and when it's 'off' you are just waiting for it to be 'on' again. The next avalanche. That is what it's like, Mr Vowells. You can't enjoy the quiet. It's like a loaded sort of quiet. Loaded with apprehension. Shires Housing Association say we're entitled to the Quiet Enjoyment of Our Home. It says so in our residents' charter. We've tried talking to Shires but they just say 4 Pennycott is nothing to do with them any more. They just ask if we've tried mediation or contacting yourselves at the council.

I can hear Mrs Trago yelling at the kids now. A barrage of F words exploding from her mouth to their target. 'Get to your fucking room this minute, you little fucking shit!' It's got to the point where me and Sandy welcome it when she—or the Trago dad— bellow and roar at their scarred-for-life kids. They're out of control. The parents as well as the kids. Barking and shouting and cursing is their default mode. They're like a family from those programmes they have about parenting that seem to be sprouting up on our TV screens on a regular basis, except there's no en suite psychologist to clean them up. I want to put the kids on mute. Especially that Bailey. He's the one making the most noise. I've seen him from the back window yelling his brothers' names at the top of his voice in that heavy throaty accent and no parent telling him not to. It's no good. We're going to have to go round there and say something. I don't know whether to call over the fence to Mrs Trago. I think she's out the back at the moment—there are wafts of cigarette smoke and Persil heading for our garden. If it was a lower fence it would be easier. Then I wouldn't have to climb up the steps to the back gate to see over. But I'm glad it's not a lower fence and that I don't have to *see* the Trago kids on a daily basis. It's bad enough hearing them. It's half-term and most of the other children from Pennycott are out and about enjoying the fair weather. You *stick* people in these houses and they can't afford to go out. It's too expensive for them. There's no thought behind your actions. Your colleagues didn't even *know* these were shared ownership properties. Or bother to do their research. Your colleague Mr Hope-Gapp said there was nothing underhand in what the council did and that any private landlord can buy up a property and let it to whom he wants. But it is different. He knows it's different. A landlord would most likely let it to professional working people. I'm not prejudiced. I have always been sympathetic to homeless people and buy my *Big Issues*. But I didn't even know these were 'special category' people until they drew attention to themselves and got us asking questions. Sandy and I have always believed everyone should have a home but our health is fragile. We're vulnerable people, Sandy with his MS and me with my Generalised Anxiety and Agoraphobia and the rest of it. I received my Disability Allowance Form through the post today, it's up for renewal, but I don't even feel up to doing it, all that form-filling. I was too terrified even to open it, if the truth be told. I knew it was from them, the DWP, and my stomach roiled and lurched, and I handed it to Sandy.

In fact, I can't even think to write *this*. This entry. The noise is like gunfire. They're costing me a small fortune in earplugs.

We've just been round there—me and Sandy. As soon as Mrs Trago opened the door on us she said, 'Oh I can't handle this—it's the *holidays!*' meaning this is what kids do in the holidays. They blast and explode all over the house and we should put up and shut up. Then she turned on the kids, shouting: 'See why I shout at you to stop! It's not for nothing! These are from next door!' This made us feel about two feet tall as you can imagine. Sandy —ever-the-diplomat — thought quickly. It's her nerves,' he said indicating me with a small head gesture in my direction. (I didn't mind him patronizing me—we'd talked about the various tacks we could take before going round there, except by the time I was angry enough to go round there, all the tacks had flown the nest). 'I'm not well either, my love,' came back the reply from Mrs Trago. 'I've just come out of hospital.' There was no evidence of what she could have been in hospital for, though she looked more scrawny of face and neck above her FCUK T-shirt and her pale grey trackies. Sandy said, 'I have MS—and Carrie here—she suffers with her mental health.' We hadn't planned on that one but once he'd said it I didn't mind. People have a fear of mental health and if that put the fear of God into her—that I might behave unpredictably—then so be it.

But as a result of our visit she's turned the kids outside, which means playing in the car park and running round the block with the other local kids. It's no better. It's just transferred the problem from inside to out. I think all that sugar's got a lot to do with it. Their faces are always swollen with some sweet or other. Coke cans are always hissing open. But I'm the one shouting now. I'm shouting at the lot of them to belt up. I'm glad that Edith is absent next door because I wouldn't want her hearing me sinking to the level of the Tragos. There goes Macklin—second-to-oldest—riding his bike standing up, treading the pedals up and down until he gets some momentum, spitting as he goes. Maybe all that gobbing is to do with his chest. There is this wheeze in his voice, which makes me wonder, Mr Vowells, if they're getting all the care and attention they clearly need. I don't mean from their parents who clearly don't know how to parent but from you and your colleagues down at the Town Hall. You have to give Families in Need of Assistance some assistance. Not just a house. Maybe there is stuff going on behind the scenes, which we don't know about. We'd like to think so—me and Sand.

But with the kids out—the Tragos are now playing their music loud. Not too loud so's you'd complain, but I can hear the bass. I won't pound on the wall. You've got to give people the benefit of the doubt.

*

'We used to play our music loud,' Sandy says, looking over Carrie's shoulder at what she's written.

'Yeah, but the flat above was empty most of the time.'

Though it's fair to say that many a time their ceiling or floor or wall would be knocked upon for quiet. They couldn't understand it, then. Carrie thinks they maybe getting their comeuppance. Their karma. What goes round comes round. All that.

Sandy turns his mind to the day's Sudoku, drawing them each a large grid with the given numbers. It helps them, to become absorbed in the world between those little squares. The enlarged grids mean there's room in every square to write out the possible numbers and then rub them out as necessary. Sandy is slower than Carrie, more methodical, whereas she rushes at it, only to find she has duplicate nines or fours or twos in a row or square or column, which throws the whole thing out.

She puffs with annoyance at the television in the background. 'Where is this place— New*cass*el?' She notes how most newsreaders have ridden this bandwagon. She thinks how, along with New*cass*el, we now also have Isrull. She wonders why they can't leave well alone. She wonders whether the people of Newcastle have changed the habit of a lifetime for this Pronunciation Correctness or whether they would agree that the new way is, after all, the old and right way.

Sandy is lost in his Sudoku. Can't be a One, Two, Three, could be a Four, can't be a Five.

Sandy regards his numbered grid with satisfaction. 'Done it.'

If only she just had numbers to fill in, Carrie thinks as she reluctantly picks up her Disability Living Allowance form. She, along with so many fellow online campaigners, regrets how this benefit is being phased out and being replaced with Personal Independence Payment. The powers-that-be always rename something when they want to cut it. This is what this Welfare Reform rhetoric is all about and it's scary for people like her and Sandy. They are seeing more and more reports via social media about seriously ill people falling through the net and dying a premature death, either because their benefit payments were cut in error or because their health was so compromised by the stress of it all. Social media is where they get a lot of their news nowadays.

She knows it's better to do the DLA form a little at a time. It's daunting having to write about your medical condition and to be reminded of all your restrictions and the fact that you've had to give up your voluntary work and re-apply for this benefit. Her life these days seems to be a never-ending round of form-filling, especially if you count the homework she has to do for Anxiety Management.

She comes to the section on mental health on the DLA form, asking her to describe in her own words the things she does or cannot do, or the experiences she has had, because of her mental health. She copies down and updates what she wrote on her last form, a draft of which she has located from her folders:

I can't cope with neighbours who make a noise. I can't cope with neighbours, period. I can't cope with groups any more, or busy crowded places, like Morrison's, or busy roads or travelling in fast cars. I can't cope with shopping much of the time, not just because of feeling dizzy and swaying and fearing collapse when I'm out, or that something terrible will happen, I also get obsessed about touching coins that are covered with a multitude of germs. I can't cope with places I don't know or anything medical like seeing the doctor or the dentist. I can't cope with waiting at the doctor's. I get all agitated and panicky and the compulsions start, doing everything three times, and the doubts that I've really turned the cooker off or unplugged the iron even though I saw myself doing it and repeated to myself 'I'm turning the switch off and I'm pulling the plug out of the socket'. Then there's all the germs in the surgery. I take my hand gel with me but you know coughs and sneezes spread diseases. I can't cope with official engagements or places with no escape, or too much pressure. Or entertaining visitors. Or having too many things to think about. Or environmental stress, like flickering lights, VDUs etc. Or sitting on rickety chairs without arms, especially in public places.

Sandy is chuckling. About the chairs. He knows what she means but to anyone else it sounds barking, he says. Isn't that the idea? she says. Not if it reads as a comedy, he replies.

She rolls her head back. The point is the Tragos are making her ill again. The noise is preventing her from even filling out her DLA form properly. If she loses her benefit it will be their fault. She had to go to a tribunal to get it in the first place. In the notes that were prepared for her appeal, there was a nasty paragraph embedded in the middle. *Miss Cornish has been able to go into great detail and at considerable length about her problems. As she has such insight into her claimed problem, no doubt she will gain a good deal of suitable help from the local Mental Health Team to overcome her problems very quickly.* So loaded, the gun could have fired any moment. She and Sandy were both disgusted. Firstly with the word 'claimed' and the implication that it was all just a fabrication. Secondly, the idea that having insight somehow lessened the severity of your condition to such an extent that you could (thirdly) get over it very quickly (if, indeed, it existed at all). At least now she knows it isn't personal. At least now she knows, via social media, that this is one of the many tricks they play on claimants to undermine them, to make them look like the fraudulent people the media says they are. Back then, when she first read those notes, there was no social media, and so it seemed intensely personal.

She stares out the window. As if all the benefits stuff wasn't bad enough without next door on top of everything else. The ten-year-old, Mason—the oldest of the Trago boys— is out there standing on a wall in a baseball cap. Previous governments have talked about hoods and baseball hats and banning them from precincts and public places. Not that she goes to precincts on account of all that flickering and visual noise which is what she was referring to on her DLA form. But she doesn't like that sort of rhetoric. It comes from the same place as people attacking those on benefits and calling them scroungers. Disabled people, once immune and protected, are now being increasingly targeted, people in wheelchairs attacked and accused of faking their disabilities. It is frightening for her and Sandy: for Sandy because he has a stick, making his disability visible, and for her because her conditions are invisible and therefore not believed to exist.

*

Day Twelve

Years fly but days drag if that makes any sense. It's hard getting from hour to hour when you're suffering. I didn't sleep well last night. I won't lie and say that the Trago kids are loud at night, they're not, they're quiet in a repressed, bullied way, but that doesn't stop my noisy heart, my noisy head, my noisy thoughts. Because you have to get an idea, Mr Vowells, of the effect all this has on people's health since Environmental Health is your speciality and my health is suffering as a result of my environment. The noise doesn't have to be constant for the health effects to be. The noise is a pest and when you get pests you call in the Pest Control.

So I was wide awake and I heard a train go by. The delayed 23.25 from Plymouth probably. We lay back to front—me and Sandy—and front to back, and then back to back, though not front to front. You can't sleep front to front. This went on several times throughout the night until Sandy went to sleep in the spare room. His MS means he sometimes gets leg spasms at night and doesn't wish to disturb me. We used to be so much more tactile where now we're just plain irritable. But I knew if I didn't get off to sleep soon I'd need the toilet and as soon as you put that idea in your head you talk your body into it. So I quit pretending I didn't want to go and relieved myself. I wanted to flush the chain but I thought it'd wake Sandy who I could hear snoring in the spare room so I went back to bed. But I could feel the compulsion coming back. I had to get up again and touch the loo chain three times before getting back into bed. Then I got up again and touched the loo chain another three times. Back to bed again before the final three taps on the chain.

But I can't cope if that comes back again in a big way. I had it bad once, before I met Sandy. It was after my relationship with Iain broke down. Well, not broke down exactly. Iain discovered he was gay, and once he made that admission, his uncertainties and insecurities disappeared. He met a guy and they went to Goa. I could have gone with them, that was made clear, but Goa was never a goer, not with my travel fears. But me and Iain— we'd looked out for each other: I'd helped him on difficult days, he'd helped me. Then he was gone, and I couldn't walk on the cracks on the pavement and I had to reach the lamp-post before the next car passed and so it went on until it took me over an hour to leave the house because I didn't believe the plugs were out or the door locked. Sometimes I even put the plugs back in, just so that I could feel them being pulled out, and that might sound crazy, Mr Vowells, but when I had the business with the loo chain last night I got this sinking feeling, and Trisha at Anxiety Management says, 'watch out for that rising or sinking feeling'. I had to take one of my Diazepams last night so I could sleep.

Today the Trago kids have been screaming round the block again. Oh that Bailey. If there was only a volume control at the side of his mouth. On all of their mouths. Or a zipper. But at the moment it's like the zip's broken and as fast as you try and close it it keeps coming open at the other end. Filth leaking out. The other local kids are getting dragged into the fray. Sandy went out earlier waving his walking stick. Not threateningly, you understand, Mr Vowells. 'Would you kids mind—?' was all he said. 'Could you play somewhere else—? I'm trying to make a phone call and I can't hear myself.' One of the other kids, Eden I think she's called, did say sorry. So they moved on for a while. But they are kids and they forget very quickly when absorbed in their world and in less than half an hour they were back. I swung open the door just as the five-year-old Bailey was holding his backside out to other kids and shouting 'kiss my arse'. Five years old! Then Eden, aged six or seven, started doing the same. It's all imitation with these kids, they see one doing it and they think it's clever. But this Eden is from a nice family, even if they are a bit hug-a-tree, and if her mum could only have seen her doing that...and so I said to Eden, I said 'Would you like me to have a word with your mother?' Well, that was enough to send her packing. Except what kids don't realize is that adults don't like to report a child's misdeeds to its parents— especially if you don't know those parents very well, or if those parents always have a nice 'hello' for you when you pass them in the road and have taught you at Yoga Class. It's just as well the kids don't realize that you've no intention of carrying out your threats. Mind you, Eden's parents are so right-on, they probably don't believe in curbing free play. Nevertheless, Eden and the nicer girls vanished after I'd issued my warning, leaving the Trago gang and the less nice kids to run amok. The noise levels crept up again and so did my blood pressure and this time I had no patience. I opened the door and shouted at them all to Get Lost. They stared at me, frozen like statues for a second, before clearing off.

But it shouldn't be our responsibility—mine and Sandy's—to police the estate, to tell other people's children where they can and can't play. Their parents should do that in keeping with the neighbourhood charter.

Moments later, I heard Mrs Trago bawling at her kids to come in. 'MACKLIN! BAILEY! Why do I have to fucking shout at you twenty-four hours seven!' She can't even get the slang right, poor woman. I say, poor woman, because I do feel sorry for her at times, with her poor health and all those kids—and I would feel more sorry for her if she wasn't my neighbour and her stresses hadn't become my stresses. But instead I stood in our doorway and in a loud voice said, 'Bad language. The first refuge of the inarticulate.' I don't know if Mrs Trago heard, it was half meant for her ears, half not. The half not was just me venting my frustration. I can't be logical about this, Mr Vowells. Or planned. Or clear-thinking. There's nothing logical or planned or clear-thinking about being driven up the pole. Sand is afraid I'm having another episode. That's what they call them these days, don't they? Episodes. One of those euphemisms for madness. Maybe I am having an episode. Maybe I'm right in the throes of one. I'm waiting for someone to say—my mother or Sandy's brother, Ken, or our sister-in-law, Dot—'You're not as you were, Carrie. You don't do the same things or have the same energy as you did.' But the tragedy is no-one's even noticed. Instead, when my mum learned that I'd had to give up my voluntary work at the Blue Cross charity shop all she said was, 'In our day, we longed for opportunities like these—going to work, and a choice of good jobs.'

She's right, of course. My life is nothing but a trail of wasted opportunities.

But all I can think is roll on Monday when the kids are back at school.

*

The following day, Carrie phones Ruth Hart from Shires Housing Association, who goes by the title of Residents' Participation Officer. Carrie's had occasion to meet Ruth Hart, when Ruth was new to the post and wanted residents' involvement with the drafting of the charter and suchlike. Ruth used to live in Liverpool and they had a friendly chat about that. Ruth seemed bubbly—her blue eyes smiling and inviting you into their confidence. So when Carrie phones Ruth about the unacceptable noise from the Pennycott kids, she expects to get Ruth's support.

'I had kids running and shouting round the block yesterday for four hours,' she says, waiting for the empathic tones of Ruth. 'It was on and off between four and eight o'clock.'

'Four and eight o'clock? So that's not late at night or anything, is it? The children have to play somewhere.'

'They didn't use to be like this. There was a whole gang of them.'

'Oh I expect it's just children playing who've grown up together.'

'Hullo? They haven't grown up together—and this isn't just playing!' (Carrie is virtually in tears by now.

What does this woman know? When did she last visit Pennycott?) 'I know what playing is, playing cooperatively, that's how the kids used to play here. But this place is now cluttered with kids, tearing around and stirring up other kids.'

'So what do you want me to do about it?'

Ruth's unsupportive and defensive stance throws Carrie. 'The charter,' Carrie says. 'It says things in the charter about parents being responsible for their kids.'

'So the charter is to help residents help themselves rather than having to contact us all the time. If you think there's a problem, why not have a polite word with the parents?'

You're having a larf encha is the phrase that plays in Carrie's head.

Ruth then says, 'So it sounds like a clash of lifestyles to me—your neighbours have got kids and you haven't,' at which point Carrie is shaking so much she hands the phone over to Sandy to put one over on Ruthless Heartless Ruth Hart, because it's *not* kids per se. Plenty of their other neighbours have got kids—(tell her that, Sandy, she says, pulling his strings from the sidelines)—but Ruth seems to have this horribly Politically Correct notion that all kids are blameless, guiltless, truly wonderful specimens of the human race. The value on children seems to have soared to an unreasonable level as far as Carrie's concerned. When she was a child it was adults who were respected. Now that she's an adult it's kids that everyone has to respect. Carrie can't help feeling that she's missed out along the way.

'Patronizing woman,' Sandy says as he comes off the phone. 'And as you know I have no time for people who begin every other sentence with that ubiquitous and redundant little 'so'. Ugh.' He shudders.

Carrie smirks. 'Yes, I got the 'so' prefix too.'

'She also blathered on about us being sensitive to noise.'

'Cheeky mare. What was that you were saying about pacifists?'

'I told her that's like a violent man telling a pacifist that he's too peaceful. That shut her up. Don't worry about it, Carrie. She's just another Trendy Wendy.'

*

Day Thirteen

The main headline today is that I'm back on 20 mls of Seroxat after an awful weekend—I've tried a whole range of this class of anti-depressants including Prozac (that made me more jittery) and Lustral, and one beginning with C (which made my lip swell) but Seroxat's the one that took the edge off things last time I needed it. I said to my GP, 'I'm being driven mad by noise,' and then I burst into tears. Tears are never far away, nowadays. But I make no apologies for them. They are just there. In-your-face. Or on-my-face to be precise. My doctor handed me a tissue and when I'd blotted them I said, 'Can I have a prescription for Seroxat and will you write me a letter that I can send to the council about the effects it's having on my health?' and my GP said she would put a letter in the post. As I came out of the surgery I squeezed a ton of antibacterial hand gel and slathered it all over my fingers. But I am now happy to be sharing my head with Seroxat Sid again. Seroxat Sid sounds much more funky than Seroxat Sue. Seroxat Sue sounds too much like a neurotic whinger who needs to get out more.

But I am so frazzled through lack of sleep (only 3-4 hours a night). All I crave is peace and quiet and the restored balance in my head. I just can't cope with this level of disturbance every weekend and every school holiday. And this morning (Monday) I heard the tornado of screeching yelping kids when I thought they'd be back at school. I can't *believe* they're not back at school after putting up with it for what seems an eternity. I thought at least I'd get some salvation at last—the Monday after half-term. Why is she keeping them off school? I said to Sandy. Hasn't she been driven mad enough by them herself this past ten days? So I phoned the local authorities to find out if the schools had gone back and there was mention of Inset Days at certain schools, which is short for In-Service Training Days, I believe. *Training Days*—did you ever hear such baloney?

I know that Mrs Trago was being sent loopy by her brood because doors were slamming. 'She's having a bad door day,' I said to Sand. Then I started slamming our doors even louder, just so she'd know what it was like having your whole house shake, but Sandy said not to. He said people like her don't hear noise any more, they've grown so acclimatized to it and the only person who was suffering was him by having two sets of doors slam. But, Mr Vowells, this is what it can drive you to. It can make you resort to their level. A taste of their own medicine. See how they like it. Serves 'em right. That sort of mentality, and Sandy and I are above that. You see, Mr Vowells, this, what we're suffering, is causing us alarm and distress, and I thought we were supposed to be protected from anything causing us alarm and distress. But we don't feel very protected.

On Saturday I was in the back garden pruning the forsythia and the leaves of the Japanese anemones, which are rampant at this time of year, when I noticed one of the net curtains flapping in one of the upstairs bedrooms next door. (It's the only room where there's a proper curtain. Downstairs in their sitting room, if you walk past it late in the evening, you can see these makeshift tartan blankets over the windows, lit-up from behind. Sometimes they're still there in the morning which makes me wonder, Mr Vowells, why the council didn't provide curtains. I know it's not your area—your area being Environmental Health—but surely your colleagues Mr Hope-Gapp or Ms Fletcher could have seen to the basics?) Anyway, I heard this voice from behind the net curtain carrying on a conversation with one of the neighbourhood girls down below. 'I like the flowers, *not*,' said the voice. I couldn't tell if it was the oldest boy Mason or the seven-year-old Macklin, already with the crack in his voice. The girl, Megan, with a fabric flower on either side of each ear got drawn into the fray by the taunting voice behind the curtain. 'Bailey, Bailey, the bells of Old Bailey!' she shouted up at the window, and then giggled to her friend. 'Shut it, you tramp,' said the voice behind the flapping curtain in an accent he shouldn't have grown into yet. The girls carried on playing down below, and every so often I could hear various obscenities coming from the curtain: Fat Cow and Lesbian Slags among them. I suppose he felt he had power behind that gauze, like a bride does behind her veil, seeing but not seen. Though he's far from anyone's idea of a bride. But Mr Vowells, Sandy and I are open-minded, liberal people, we've been around and seen all sorts and been guilty of a few misplaced expletives ourselves when provoked but it isn't the sort of language we expect around here—least of all from a kid as young as seven (or even five if indeed it was Bailey.)

And on Sunday, Sandy saw Macklin holding his middle finger up to another boy. 'Kiss that,' he said. It would be funny if it wasn't such a sad reflection of our times. Sad that their parents condone it or don't even notice it. They're teenagers already these seven-year-olds, it's frightening. But a whole clutter of local kids were racing and screaming round the block, the Trago kids having stirred them all up: stirred up all those kids with the potential for raucousness given the right—or rather wrong—company. That's most kids if you think about it. Most kids will run riot given half the chance. I shouted at them to GO AND PLAY SOMEWHERE ELSE. I shouted at them to STOP SCREAMING OUTSIDE MY FRONT DOOR. They did stop, stunned for a second. Then a few minutes later they were back. If only there'd been a mute button so we could switch off the relentless thud thud thud, clatter clatter clatter, slam slam slam at annoyingly close intervals. It wasn't outdoors any more but inside. They were *all* in there next door, I swear. That house is a magnet for all the local kiddie population. It's like being next door to an adventure playground, minus the supervisors. Well, that was enough, Mr Vowells. There must have been ten kids in there running amok. Enter Seroxat Sid. He couldn't help myself. His fists did a great tattoo of knocks on the party wall. He could hear how hollow the wall is. The house just isn't suitable for the purpose—the new purpose assigned to it by your colleagues at the council.

    So on the way to the doctors, Sandy put a note through their front door saying that we needed to discuss things in view of the structure. It was a friendly sort of note and Sandy signed both our names and put our phone number on it but they haven't responded. But that reminds me, Mr Vowells, I will phone you tomorrow and see where you are with the soft furnishings and I can also let you know about the latest problems we've been having and update you on the diary.

*

The following day, on her way back from the shops, Carrie sees the O'nions woman from Number 5 who she's heard going by the name of Louann. As Carrie's about to descend the small flight of steps between Number 4 and Number 5 Pennycott, she sees the O'nions woman through the railings tending some plants in the corner of her garden. Plants say a lot about people. Having responsibility for flowers and caring about what happens to them speaks volumes about your attitude to the neighbourhood in general. The Tragos don't have plants or flowers—botanical life wouldn't stand an earthly against such a tearaway bunch.

The O'nions woman is aged about thirty. Today her auburn hair is tied up in a small ponytail, shaped like a C. She's wearing shorts and sandals. She looks up as Carrie passes. She doesn't smile right away, then proffers a nod, her mouth lifting slightly at the ends into one of those smiles that doesn't look like a smile. Carrie wonders if Louann O'nions is disturbed by the Tragos too—though, of course, she has the buffer of the passageway and steps in between. Still, she must have heard the Trago kids. She is still next door to them, even if the walls aren't adjoined. Carrie would like to ask her but all she manages is 'Are you settling in OK?' to which the O'nions woman replies 'Yes fine' curtailing the conversation somewhat. Then again, the O'nions woman is a newcomer to Pennycott and probably doesn't want to get off to a bad start with a reputation as a whinger. But Louann O'nions looks like someone who might be on Carrie's wavelength and this possibility gives her confidence to probe a little further. 'Are you bothered by the noise?' she proffers, gesturing her head almost imperceptibly in the direction of the Tragos, hoping to invite Louann O'nions into her confidence, a shared ally against the daily anarchy between them.

Louann O'nions stands, trowel in one hand, a few weeds in the other, as she briefly ponders Carrie's question. 'Well...kids will be kids, if that's what you mean,' she says, before resuming her attention to her flower beds.

But her reply has further boosted Carrie's position. Of course, Louann O'nions wouldn't want to openly complain, would she? It's not as if she and Carrie are bosom buddies. But Carrie's sure Louann will have seen in her a fellow confidante and, as she's dumping the shopping on her kitchen worktop, she decides to phone Environmental Health.

Sandy is out getting some massage and oxygen treatment at the MS Centre in Exeter. Carrie could wait until he's back home, later in the afternoon, but she will only get herself more worked up. It was all she could do to go out to the nearest shops on her own, the way she's been feeling lately, though the Seroxat will kick in fully soon—two to three weeks they say, but she thinks she may be feeling the benefit already. Whatever it is, it spurs her to pick up the phone. But once she's been put through to Environmental Health and asks to speak to Mr Vowells the girl on the other end says, 'I'm sorry he's at lunch—would you like to phone back at two o'clock?' So Carrie phones back at ten past two and the girl on the other end says, 'He's on the other line at the moment—would you like to hold?' This is what she must include on her DLA form—if she hasn't already—the *waiting*. Waiting gets her in a stew. If she can just get things over with, it's never quite so bad. 'I could get him to call you back?' says the girl. 'No—I'll hold for a bit.' (Waiting around on the other end of the line isn't as bad as waiting around half the afternoon for them to call you back.)

Finally she gets to speak to Mr Vowells. 'Hello, how are things?' he says, like her doctor might say. She just manages to prevent her tongue from saying 'never better'.

'Terrible,' she says, though the conviction in her voice seems to have slipped now that the kids have finally gone back to school. Part of her wants to get on with life and forget all the woes and complaints, part of her wants to play it all down because she's a free-living person, she doesn't like all this bother, but experience has shown her that it'll only happen again and then she'll kick herself for not taking action when she had the chance and, more importantly, the energy. There's a tendency to let it lie once the worst has subsided when in fact that's just the time when you need to be doing something. Sometimes, right in the thick of it is not the best time when energy is low, tempers high, and articulation minimal.

'Last week was half-term—and we didn't get a moment's peace.' She gives a shaky sigh. 'What's the latest on the soft furnishings?'

'Soft furnishings?'

'You know—when you and your colleague came to knock on our walls earlier in the year and heard how the sound travels—you said you would get some more soft furnishings for that house.' (She doesn't really want to be going down this road, it is tantamount to putting the problem solely down to structure, rather than the behaviour of the tenants).

'I'm afraid that's up to the housing department. I did say I couldn't promise anything.'

Carrie tries to fight the sinking feeling. 'When you went round to our neighbours' house that time—what did you say to them again?'

'I told them they have a right to enjoy their home just like anyone else but to consider their neighbours and to try and keep the noise down—though it is difficult with children—'

'I'm—we're continuing with the diary—like you asked us to do.'

'Good.'

'And we put a note through next door—a friendly note saying we needed to come to an agreement over noise levels in the light of your findings over the structure of the house—'

'Oh yes?'

'They've totally ignored it.'

'Well, sometimes it's best to have a friendly word face to face. Notes can be a bit intimidating.'

Carrie falls quiet, not wanting it to end at such an inconclusive juncture.

'I suggest you carry on monitoring the situation as you're doing.'

'OK. Bye.'

Her OK and the Bye were short. Monotone. Brusque. Both of them crammed with growing dissatisfaction and resentment at feeling brushed-off.

*

Day Fourteen

This morning, Sunday, I felt like hell on legs, the way you do after a sleepless night...Sandy's snoring didn't help...I feel I could divorce him on the grounds of unreasonable behaviour when his snoring keeps me awake...and the way he rocks to one side to break wind, usually in my direction...You shouldn't read too much into the fact that I haven't done the diary this last week, Mr Vowells...I just haven't been able to... Maybe I'm becoming desensitized to the noise, though in some ways I'm becoming more sensitized because it takes less now for me to get stressed...like my defences are weakened...and I had a sleepless night because of having to go back and touch the loo chain three times whenever I went to the loo in the night and the going back and tapping woke me up good and proper, hence the sleeplessness...I was going to write this out again, without the three dots between sentences but I'm aware that they come from the same place as the loo chain thing...it's something about threes and feeling safe if you've done something three times instead of once...third time lucky is what they say, though Trisha at the Anxiety Group says that it's part of my OCD...I may be obsessive-compulsive, but I'm not mad...I have insight...I am an intelligent, educated woman...though the insight thing was used against me when I was first turned down for Disability Living Allowance...it's just that the Threes make me feel like I'm averting disaster...that if horrible things happen to me...to us...then it won't be through anything I did or didn't do...in short, it won't be my fault for doing things only once, instead of getting them covered three times...we live in house Number 3 and before moving in Clo told us all the numerology stuff about Threes and it seemed Threes were good and lucky, though now it seems a whole lot of hooey...Clo is my friend, by the way...She and Sofe are my two best friends...I met them through a Sufferers of Agoraphobia and Panic Attacks group or SOAPS for short...must be over ten years ago now...well, actually, I only met Sofe there, and Clo was Sofe's best friend but Clo wasn't able to make it to any of the meetings at that time...I didn't meet her until later...but as I'm an only child, they are like sisters to me, I suppose...not that we look alike...Clo with her short reddish hair and glasses is much shorter than me and although Sofe has long hair like me, it's straighter and dark brown where mine is sort of gold with kinks.

(When the sentence ends though, I can't have the three dots because that's like something open-ended and unfinished...and I am superstitious about that...a lot of this OCD stuff stems from superstition...it's like turning off the TV in the middle of a horrid news item, when people are dying and being blown up...I can't do that, because then I'd be left with negative images and something terrible might befall us...I know it's daft really, but that's why I wait for the news to finish, because it usually ends on some light-hearted item or the weather...but even then, if the weather looks gloomy that's a bad omen so I have to switch over...I flick through the channels until there's something light-hearted or funny before switching it off and then it'll all be OK.)

But this morning when I opened the front door, just to check out the weather, I'm sure I saw some pee on our doorstep...Bailey, I bet...the sort of thing a five-year-old would do, thinking it's dead funny...I wouldn't be surprised if Mrs Trago told her kids to go and do it on our front doorstep...She probably said 'go and piss on their doorstep to annoy them'...I know a kid's been there because I saw the print of a small trainer in this wee, though Sandy says it could be something leaking from the porch, or a cat...that's the sort of person Sandy is, you see, Mr Vowells...thinking the best of people.

There is so much dropped litter about too...torn packets of junky sweets...I know the litter annoys Fiona, the mother of Eden, who lives a few doors along...and other residents are starting to notice the deterioration of the neighbourhood...and a gang of kids instigated by the Trago Gang are dragging bits of scaffolding round the block...they pick them up like they're toys...Sandy's had to go out twice to tell them to put them down because they are dangerous and not toys.

This weapon-brandishing all started when those Trago kids moved in next door...the other local children have also started running around with sticks which they bang on fences and doors in what I call destructive and not constructive play, in spite of Ruth Heartless's comments...and I've been thinking, Mr Vowells, about what you said the other day when we talked, about how you told our neighbours that they have a right to enjoy their home, which would be fine if you hadn't missed out the vital word 'quiet'...because that is what it says in our Residents' Charter...the right to *quiet* enjoyment of our home...but in the wrong hands, missing out that vital word could be misinterpreted, and if you'll forgive me for saying this, Mr Vowells, could even be perceived as encouraging our neighbours to make as much noise as they like because these sorts of people think that is what is meant by enjoyment of your home and Sod the Neighbours...I'm sure you didn't mean it like that, but I'm equally sure that's how it'll have been interpreted.

*

Carrie is following all the Welfare Reform News on social media and how it will affect people like her and Sandy. She would have thought that after two years of the Con Dems she would cease to be shocked by some of their nasty little antics. But on the news again tonight, it was announced that the Prime Minister was on the side of workers 'rather than those making a living on benefits'. Sandy screws his face up: 'Is this unbiased reporting? Making a living on benefits?' Carrie agrees. Maybe the reporter is only repeating the words of the Prime Minister but they both know that a single unemployed person aged over 25 years gets around £71 per week to live on (excluding housing and council tax benefits), and that has only gone up very recently because of inflation. It was previously £67 a week. They both know that on this amount, said Job Seeker has to pay for food, fuel, and other utilities, such as water, phone calls and TV license, at the bare minimum. And this is week in, week out. Carrie wants to scream at the TV. 'How the fuck is this *making a living*?' If she thought the Prime Minister lived in la-la land it might be slightly less pernicious but they both know he knows exactly what he's doing. He's playing to the gallery in the form of the populist right-wing press who get their funds by and large from the Tory Party and their associates. She and Sandy both know that the baying mob have already been whipped up to think that benefit recipients get too much because they've all seen the screeching headlines about benefit caps of 26K. 26K? Sweet Jesus, she and Sandy know that most people on benefits get under 10K. In the few thousand cases where claimants get 26K, the families don't see this money—it goes in rent to profiteering landlords, but the PM and his tricksters would rather blame the claimant than the landlords for the rising rents they have failed to regulate. It is all calculation and manipulation to get the hoi polloi onside—and it suits the Con Dems' ideological agenda if the masses believe benefits claimants all get 26K. Carrie and Sandy and their fellow armchair campaigners on social media know all too well that the government are not too fussed on presenting accurate facts...

She and Sandy are, as a result, filled with dread at the prospect of being migrated from Incapacity Benefit to Employment & Support Allowance. The forms have all changed, the test is becoming more and more stringent, claimants aren't believed, the papers are full of them all faking it, and the private companies working on behalf of the Department of Work & Pensions have targets. The government say there are no targets but everyone knows there are. Carrie thinks again with a growing sense of dread of the letter which will come to strip her of her income: an intrusion through her letterbox—like a rape. She wishes they could have a post box at the end of the drive, like they do in the USA. Then it would be less intrusive. Then again, maybe it is just as bad, taking the long walk of fear to the box on a post, dreading what you might find when you get there. Just moving the rape from inside to out...

She knows from Clo and Sofe and her friends on social media that everybody in her situation has brown envelope phobia, that at least she is not alone.

January 2013

The hospital have operated on the woman's head injury, removing a clot. Her family and friends have been told it's critical but stable. She lies barely conscious with a bandage round her head and tubes in her nose. No mother wants to see her daughter like that. Her father has gone home to get some of her things. Her mother is in a daze as her cup of tea remains untouched in the hospital café. It is a gloomy day outside: Christmas a receding memory, spring still a long way off. She knows her daughter is a fighter. She has to believe it. She remembers the time when she was a child and developed acute appendicitis. Her face was all flushed and she had a fever.

Her mother has no concept or understanding of neighbour conflicts. Neither she nor her husband would get in touch with the authorities if they had neighbour problems. Her generation rallies, they help out neighbours in need, but they are a dying breed. Younger generations are different. The old Biblical commandment of Love Thy Neighbour has been ditched by the younger folk who expect so much more. Or is it so much less? They don't want to know or help their neighbours, they don't seem to want to be community-minded any more…

Another prayer is said in her head, it comes automatically—even though she's not really religious. But so far, her prayers have been answered. She stares into her empty cup, with no memory of having drunk it.

July 2012

One Saturday, in early July, Carrie does a double-take at the sight through the back bedroom window.

'Sandy. Sandy, quick in here! I think they're *going*.'

'Who? What?' He appears as quickly as he can manage and flicks up the edge of the net curtain. 'Jesus blood Christ! There is a god after all.'

'Do you think they've listened to us, Sand? At the council?'

'Possibly. Maybe others have made complaints too. About the kids. And the noise. The council are probably moving them on. Well, they can't chuck them out on the street, can they? Not with all those kids.'

Carrie stands fixated at the back bedroom while the Tragos move out, just to make sure she's not dreaming it; that she's not somehow misinterpreted the situation and that perhaps they're only getting rid of old clutter and tat in a large van to make room for more.

After watching carefully and intently, she dares to believe that it's really happening: that their problems of the last six months—these problems, at least—are at an end. Shires Housing Association have put pressure to bear on the council and the council have at last listened. Alleluia. There's Logan, in the manner of his father, slinging his plastic bike into the back of the van in an effort to be helpful but creating perfect mayhem for mum and dad Trago as they climb up and down at the back of the van, shifting stuff further inside to create more space for their tacky clobber. Against her better judgement, this is how Carrie views their belongings.

On the Saturday evening, when she's sure the Tragos

have gone, Carrie peers through the front window of Number 4. She can see the mess in there—bits of litter and broken plastic and gawd knows what else. She doesn't imagine the Tragos will come back and clean it up, she secretly hopes they won't, then the council will see for themselves, they'll have the evidence because Carrie gets this feeling that they have doubted her word for some reason. But on Sunday afternoon, Carrie can hear sound in the house, like someone sweeping and brushing. And there's Mrs Trago picking up a few bits and bobs up from outside, displaying her trademark twisted thong above her jeans as she does so. They're going to leave it spick and span (they couldn't even get that right—the bastards) before returning the keys on Monday, though they have left their old mattresses in the back garden.

On the Sunday night Carrie has a dream with a recurring theme. The dream is of the house next door (always Number 4, never Edith's house) except the boundaries between the houses have somehow blurred or broken down such that Carrie finds herself able to freely wander through an adjoining door between the two houses or see over an inadequate partition which serves as a party wall. In her dreams this lack of privacy is always a cause for anxiety. It is someone else intruding on her life. Neither does it always involve the Tragos. It goes back to the original shared owners: the Zamoras. When the Zamoras first moved in, Carrie and Sandy could hear very little. If anything, more noise came from the other side, from Edith, who had a phase of slamming the back door and playing her television loud. Although alarmed by the heavy thump of Edith's door, Carrie got the feeling that it was an OCD thing with Edith, and felt a certain empathy. But then Edith had her front bedroom converted into a sitting room and the noise subsided.

Peace reigned for a short while on both sides until one day, at one of their early residents' meetings, Harry Zamora said to Carrie and Sandy, 'You don't hear our music, do you?' He asked it out of consideration in his broken English voice (he was Nicaraguan). 'No, not at all,' Carrie and Sandy chimed in unison. The meeting was good-spirited, a chance to get to know their neighbours as well as exchange notes on the newly-built Pennycott houses. (How do you get the batteries into the smoke alarms? What is that socket for on the landing? There's all this security at the front door—chains and spyholes and bolts and double locks and then—then there's the back door with diddly squat!) That was when they made their first mistake. In answering 'no' to Harry's question they were giving him carte blanche to turn his music up, and turn it up he did.

In the early days, Carrie and Sandy would respond in kind (provided Edith was out, for they didn't want to disturb an elderly neighbour) but that tactic failed. Harry either couldn't hear with his own music at such high levels, or he interpreted it as, Oh good, they obviously like to play their music loud too. And it's true, Carrie used to. She liked her music loud and proud. She didn't want music coming to her through phones over her head. She liked Out There music. She wanted everyone to hear her Killing Joke, her The The. She was one of those people who secretly went by the maxim: *My neighbours listen to good music whether they like it or not.* But having an elderly neighbour next door put paid to that and she learned to consider the needs of others. She learned that just because you love music, doesn't mean that you want other people's music at other people's times. It was the old story of when it's yours, it's music, when it's theirs, it's noise. Because what Harry and Jules Zamora played she didn't consider to be music. It was all that techno/trance stuff so loved by that strata of people a few years younger than herself who knew the different gradations and classifications. It was music to wind you up by, for not only did Harry have a quick burst of it when he came home from work, and especially on a Friday evening, he and Jules also played it into the small hours when they had their occasional all-night parties. They made a pig-awful din. It was the worst kind of music for anyone with an anxious or phobic disposition for it sounded like your heart beating twenty to the dozen inside your head. The worst thing about it was Carrie would think it was over—it tended to have lulls in the middle—then the fast thumping bass would start up again, more furious than before, punctuated by shrieks of drunken laughter. She didn't like to complain to the Zamoras though, because she'd been there. She'd been one of those playing her music loud—bang bang bang— and now she's one of those banging for quiet. She wished she and Sandy had gone round and nipped it in the bud straight away with the Zamoras, instead of being ones to keep the peace. They might have saved themselves a lot of sleepless nights. Sometimes, they would hear the odd strumming of a guitar and a general over-exuberance coming from the Zamora side: high spirited laughter and chatter which increased in volume with the amount of alcohol consumed.

Although these all night affairs were occasional and only at weekends, music and partying wasn't the only intrusion from the Zamoras. They were also great home improvers and there were great bursts of hammering and drilling as laminate floors were put in the sitting room and the smallest bedroom. In the kitchen they installed a slate floor, such that when they had their parties you could hear chairs scraping across the floor all night long. Carrie thinks that people should be able to scrape their chairs if they want but equally she thinks that other people shouldn't be hearing it and especially not from a bedroom furthest away from the source. This makes her think that the party wall (how apt a name) must be inadequate which she's no doubt will be picked up by the forthcoming sound tests, due on Tuesday. Carrie believes this to be at the root of her boundary dreams. Lives from next door spilling into her space.

'It's a territory metaphor,' Sandy says. 'That's what's at the heart of your dream. Of all of them.'

She looks to the floor where the sheets have fallen. Sheets always seem to come off around her. They did the same when she was with Iain, her gay ex who ran off to Goa with his lover. She puts it down to being a messy sleeper but maybe there's more to it. Maybe she's tossing and turning in her boundary-challenging dreams.

'Most wars are about territory, too, deep down.'

'No they're not.' She is both surprised and annoyed at Sandy's sweeping generalization. 'They're about oil and religion and all sorts of things.'

'Well, that just about covers it.'

'So what are you driving at, Sandy? That we were at war with our neighbours?'

'A cold war, you might call it. Our own little dispute.'

Carrie is angry at this suggestion as she's always thought of herself as a pacifist. She would have been for Talks, and settling disputes by Reasonable Means and Mediation if they'd been set in motion. Those aren't the weapons of a warmonger, surely.

'It's water under the bridge now, anyway, Carrie. They've gone! That's the main thing.'

He's right, there's really no need for them to be bickering, and tonight they will hopefully be able to broaden their horizons again as they watch the news, the whole news, and nothing but the news.

But the morning has barely begun before they hear distant footsteps in the house next door and plugs going on and off. The van parked outside confirms that the electrical contractors are checking the electrics. The council haven't wasted any time. Later the painters come, touching up the paintwork all ready for the new people. Carrie hasn't given much thought to the New People. They've hardly had time to draw breath, she and Sandy, though anything unknown is a cause for apprehension.

The quietness over the weekend was pure bliss, but now the new week has begun there's this disconcerting cloud hovering over the bliss as they count down to the day, very soon, surely, when they'll have new neighbours. Carrie now sits and wonders. What sort of people will they be, these new neighbours of theirs? What will they look like? How many children will they have? What intruding routines will they have? One thing's for sure, nobody could be worse than the Tragos, could they?

On the Tuesday, the man from the acoustics company—a Ludwik someone or other—calls at Carrie and Sandy's with a set of keys to next door and proceeds to set up his equipment on both sides of the party wall. He has what looks like recording equipment, a microphone and a monitor, as well as other gizmos, and says he will be measuring the background noise levels and then playing a pink noise signal through the PA in each of the rooms next door. Ludwik darts from house to house, making his signal and reading the measurements, Sandy following him round and asking him questions, and when he is perhaps three quarters of the way through there's a ring on the bell.

'I'll get it, Sandy.'

Standing in the doorway is a young woman with a baby in her arms standing beside an older woman.

'Excuse me, is this 3 Pennycott?' asks the young woman.

Carrie smiles. 'It is, yes.'

'Are you moving out?'

Carrie looks blank for a moment. 'Oh, it'll be next door you want.'

'Oh the council said it was Number 3,' says the older woman, a hint of Liverpool in her voice. 'Can we just have a peep inside your house to give us some idea?'

'Of course.' Carrie gets a good feeling about them in those few seconds. The way they smile, the consideration in their tone. 'You're welcome to have a look, though the layout is different in the two-bedroom houses than the three-bed ones.' She adds, 'But there's a guy here running some sound tests and we don't want to mess up the scientific method!'

The older woman looks a bit puzzled.

'He's just testing the soundproofing.'

'Oh Justine's dead quiet,' the older woman says of the younger woman (her daughter presumably). 'You can't even hear her television.'

This is all music to Carrie's ears as she invites the women into the hallway.

'The house next door is empty,' she says and then remembers that Ludwik has the keys. She interrupts him and asks if she can show the prospective tenants around next door, momentarily forgetting how she might be sabotaging the results in the process, but if the young woman and child are to be the new tenants and are true to their word, then the whole soundproofing issue may no longer be an issue, and the sound tests merely a formality.

Ludwik hands her the keys saying she might as well show them round while he finishes off what he's doing.

As she's walking round with the keys in her hand to Number 4, the prospective tenants eagerly at her side, it occurs to her that she's never been into the upstairs part of next door. She feels like an estate agent or someone important as she unlocks the door and shows Justine—her possible neighbour-to-be—around Number 4, her mother in tow. Justine is a fair-haired girl, early twenties, high cheek bones. A nice fresh face which lights up when she sees the kitchen. 'Oh look at the shelving! It's a good size, isn't it, mum?'

In between Justine's exclamations of approval Carrie discusses Liverpool and Crosby with Justine's mother. Justine's older brothers went to the same school as Carrie, it transpires. The smallness of the world and football teams are talked about (Justine's mother's allegiance is with the blue half of Merseyside, so they have a little banter). It is all good-natured, though Justine, southern born and bred, doesn't join in. Justine is worried that the rent is quite high, though the council have offered it to them for two, possibly four years, she says. Carrie can barely contain her joy. Two to four *years.* They look ideal neighbours, and it transpires that Justine goes to work part time, her husband full time, and mum lives locally.

Upstairs, Justine looks at the back bedroom and then lovingly at her baby girl in arms 'This is where you'll be sleeping, sweet pea.'

The following day, Carrie hears noises coming from next door: not from Number 4 but the house on the other side—Number 2—so adept is she at identifying the source. It's a non-intrusive sort of noise—the swish of a hand down the stair rail, soft footfall. But Carrie has grown so accustomed to Edith's house being empty, she'd forgotten about listening out for sound on that side.

Now she has another unknown to worry about. It is all upheaval. She goes to the back bedroom, overlooking the car park, and sure enough there's a removal van and men carrying boxes and furniture into Edith's old house. She and Sandy must have missed Edith moving out— probably done while they were at her parents' house one time. She scans the straggle of people in the car park for who might be her new neighbours. A woman appears at the back gate: blond, full, middle-aged. Yes, that is probably her. Carrie sees her smile at one of the removal men as he negotiates a three-piece-suite down the steps. A smile is good. The smile looked friendly. She hears the woman say a few words—the words and accent indistinct: another good sign, although Carrie would like to hear the words themselves. Words provide clues as to whom you're dealing with and what to expect. She thinks she may have heard the word daughter. Sandy catches her eavesdropping.

'I wondered if we should go round there, Sand, and introduce ourselves.'. This is not something she normally would do, she is normally the kind of person to hold back and wait for others to make the first move. But Trish from Anxiety Management says it's empowering to be proactive. It would also help to glean some information about the woman. Has she a husband or partner? Will she be out at work a lot? Information is power. Information gives control over what and who you're dealing with.

'Can't do any harm,' Sandy agrees.

'Start as we mean to go on, eh? Create a good first impression.'

They decide to strike while the iron is hot.

After tapping the front door of Number 2, they stand back a bit so as not to look too in-your-face.

Carrie feels an inner lurch of anxiety as the door opens but over-thinking can get you into trouble so she launches straight in.

'We're from next door. I'm Carrie and this is Sandy. Just thought we'd pop by and say hi and see if you need anything?' Carrie is taken aback by her own forthrightness, but something about new situations can be liberating, before they have set into old routines and lines you cannot or dare not cross. The blond woman beams—her largeness quite attractive, close up—and holds out a hand for them each to shake. 'Oh nice to meet you. I'm Priss,' she says. 'Come on in. Excuse all the boxes and stuff, won't you? The men have just gone to pick up the next load.' She smiles. 'My mother's sorting them out at the other end.'

Carrie follows Priss through the narrow hall into Edith's old living room, which is the mirror image of theirs: cupboard door, back door and window all on the wrong side—always a touch disorientating. 'So is your mother moving in with you too?'

Priss throws back her head and howls with laughter. 'Christ, no. It's just me and my youngest daughter. I do love my mum but we couldn't share a house, hun.' She shifts a couple of boxes off the three piece suite. 'Sit down and I'll make you a tea. It's so nice of you to call. I made sure I had access to the most important box with the kettle and the cups and teabags! Even got some milk open.'

As she makes their drinks and chats, Carrie starts to relax. Priss seems very friendly. Sandy asks if she's local and Priss says they lived in Paignton before but they didn't really like it there. Sandy offers her a conspiratorial grin—as if to say, who could blame her? It transpires that she's a divorcee but has virtually no contact with the father of her two girls.

While they are sipping their mugs of tea, an inquisitive look appears in Priss's green eyes all of a sudden. 'Other neighbours OK?'

Carrie and Sandy exchange glances briefly and nod.

'There's a very nice gentleman, Melvyn Styles, to your other side,' Carrie volunteers. 'There's a young couple in Number 5, they're fairly new...and we've got new neighbours moving in on the other side of us any day now, so it's all change!'

'And we're pretty quiet,' Sandy adds.

'Oh good! Nothing worse than noisy neighbours.'

This is more music to Carrie's ears. The sweetest melody.

'Or neighbours who cause trouble,' Priss adds. 'You both work then?'

Sandy raises his stick aloft: the funky black one with the white polka dots Carrie bought for him one time. 'Retired early due to ill health.'

'Oh poor you...my eldest daughter, Ellie, she's disabled. She's in a wheelchair. She has her own specially adapted flat in the town, one of the reasons why we moved over here actually...to be near to her.' She blows on her tea. 'I also have a part time job in Morrison's here.'

She turns to Carrie, as if to ask her something—maybe about her own occupational status but thinks better of it. 'Well, I suppose I better get back to unpacking my boxes,' she says, rising from her makeshift seat. 'Then the sooner I can reach the proper chairs over there!' She laughs. 'I'm telling myself this is a good way of losing weight as I'm twice the woman I was!'

As Carrie and Sandy rise to leave, Priss says, 'It's so nice meeting you...you must come over again when this is less of a bombsite!' She's looking straight into Carrie's eyes now, laying a hand on her wrist. 'I can see we're going to get on, hun. I get this feeling about people and I get a good feeling about you.'

Carrie smiles, all aglow. 'Just knock on our door if you need anything.'

She comes away, pleased at having reached out; at portraying themselves as friendly, caring neighbours. It feels good. It feels as if she's somehow loosened, like there's some slack to spare at last. Like she's in the middle of her tether, for once, rather than at the end of it, though Sandy is dubious about all the 'gut feeling' stuff once they return to their own house. 'She barely knows us.'

'Don't knock it, Sand. Things are starting to go right for us at last. Priss on one side, Justine soon on the other.'

Sandy manages a half-smile. 'I suppose.'

A few days into the changes at Number 2, Carrie feels her body uncoiling further and becomes accustomed to the faint and non-intrusive routine of their new neighbours in Edith's old house. All they've heard is what you'd expect: the usual settling in noises, like curtain rails and picture hooks being put up. Carrie catches occasional glimpses of Priss and her teenaged daughter, Bethan, who is at school during the day—though school will be breaking up for summer soon. One thing Carrie has learnt is that you're much more tolerant of noise when you like the people or know the people—you don't feel they're doing it to annoy. You don't even hear it. That's how they used to feel about the Zamoras sometimes, after they'd cleared the air over any dispute, usually involving their late-night music. It did keep her and Sandy awake at times to the extent that they had to put on the extractor fan in the bathroom and wear earplugs to get some sleep and if that failed Carrie would hammer on the wall. They were too tolerant in those days—letting it go on for a few hours, letting their sleep be assaulted, before doing anything. It was partly because Carrie and Sandy did love to play music loud themselves in the old days, so they had that understanding. But with old Edith next door, all that had to die a death.

Carrie recalls one time when she and Sandy were so pissed off with the Zamoras for partying all night, they started bashing that old drum Sandy used to play—a big African drum with a beat to wake the dead or at least the seriously hungover—when they knew the Zamoras would be sleeping off the previous night. But the thing with the Zamoras was they always apologized and they didn't mind Carrie and Sandy telling them when enough was enough. They didn't bear a grudge. If Edith was out, she and Sandy could turn their music up even louder than the Zamoras and they would get the message. They wouldn't take it personally. They could all joke about the way they could hear each others plugs and the way the cupboards banged and the drawers slammed in the kitchen, followed by promises to each other to be more careful in future. After such cosy, considerate chats, Carrie and Sandy wouldn't hear their noises as much and if they did they'd just shrug and say, live and let live, because a little goodwill went a long way. In fact, the Zamoras ended up inviting Carrie and Sandy to one of their parties. At the party, Sandy quoted what he said was a well-known maxim: *Nothing makes you more tolerant of a neighbour's noisy party than being there.*

*

Day Zero

I'm writing this in pencil as I'm sure it won't amount to anything, Mr Vowells, and it's not about our new neighbours in Number 2.

You see, I thought of the O'nions' at Number 5 like the Zamoras—a young, professional couple, only the O'nions' aren't the sort to keep you awake at night with their parties, not them. That was why we were horrified to see the note attached to Sandy's bike. Because of his MS, Sandy has this fold-up bike where you can detach the handlebars, it's handy for putting in the boot if friends or family come and we go out for a drive somewhere. Anyway, we'd been out for a drive with my folks last Saturday, and then we'd gone for a local walk, Sandy accompanying us on his bike, until he cycled home early, giving me some time with my family. My parents were using our car space, so when Sandy got back, rather than carry the bike down the steps which would have been a lot of effort for him, he put it onto the scrubby bit of land which borders our parking space and tied it to the cherry tree there. We thought nothing more of it until I went out to wave my parents off and bring in Sandy's bike. That's when I noticed the note sellotaped against it. You couldn't miss it. It read: *please move your bike from our garden, it is ruining our plants.*

My mum said, 'That's not very friendly, is it? Do you know who wrote it?'

I told her I didn't but I intended to find out. 'It's not a garden anyway!' and then I snatched the note off the bike after I'd said goodbye to my parents and showed it to Sandy. He was well miffed like me but too tired to do anything about it at that moment.

Cue Seroxat Sid. We braved the O'nions' together—Seroxat Sid and me—since the scrubby bit of land is nearest to their property.

I rapped on their door.

The O'nions guy answered.

'Did you write this note?' I asked in the deeper tones of Seroxat Sid since deep equals confidence (rather than squeaking off into girlie hysteria).

'I think my wife did,' the O'nions' guy said in an assured, well-spoken voice. Close up, I started seeing him in a different light. What I'd always thought as a pleasant, polite manner I was now seeing as snide. That smile looked smarmy, the bijou eyes, sly. 'She didn't know whose bike it was,' he added, stroking his pencil-goatee.

I was raging. 'Hullo? Sandy has MS?' I caught myself doing the 'upswing'—you know, that thing when you say something like it's a question when it isn't? Sandy hates it but it gives me confidence. I think I was smiling too, which I sometimes do when I'm angry, so I've been told. 'And his bike wasn't doing any harm to any plants?' Seroxat Sid then zoomed me off like a high-speed train before the O'nions' guy had a chance to come back at us (that is, me and Seroxat Sid).

I stewed. Sandy's bike was on a tiny bit of dry scrubby earth which, as far as I know, is communal land and doesn't even belong to the O'nions'. The bit of land in question has no plants to ruin, unless you count the ragged shrubs that the local children tear through on a daily basis (this is the legacy left by the Tragos) and anyway Sandy's bike was nowhere near anything with foliage. He's careful and considerate about where he leaves it. To think that we offered them the use of our parking space for their second car too (though now we're on it, it wasn't 'we' who made the generous offer, it was Sandy).

Anyway, yesterday (Wednesday) a chance for revenge presented itself. The O'nions' horrid gas guzzler was parked in our parking space like it was on Tuesday. I wondered why they were in our space when their own space was empty until I realized they were washing their car with a hose stretching from their garden. I realized why they were in our space, because the car spaces are slightly staggered from our properties, our space being nearer to the O'nions' property and so on, right to the end of the block. While they were indoors Seroxat Sid goaded me to put the note he'd inspired me to write onto their car. It said: SHIFT YOUR CAR FROM OUR SPACE. I came back inside having wedged said note under their windscreen and the O'nions woman came out. Whether she'd seen the note or not, she seemed to be ignoring it. Fuelled by Seroxat Sid I stomped out again then, the red rag dangling in my face. How dare she ignore my note! How dare she carry on cleaning like jack shit had happened! Her head was buried inside the car—cleaning and sweeping—and she didn't hear my 'excuse me'. When her face emerged I could see her sharp dark eyes. Choppy new haircut. Defined attributes. So I turned to him, Rick O'nions, hose in hand, my lines already rehearsed with the help of my inner persona. 'Excuse me, is it convenient for you to clean your car here?'

Yes, he said. His hose only reached the car when parked in our space (just as I'd guessed).

'Just as it was convenient for Sandy to park his bike here the other day,' I said, gesticulating victoriously to the scrubby bit of land.

I asked the O'nion female if she'd seen the note and she said she had and was going to move her car when she'd finished what she was doing. She had some front. I said to her it was on our property and if it was a driveway would she still come and park on it to which she replied 'now you're being ridiculous.'

No-one has ever disrespected our property rights in such a brazen manner before. Well, words were said. The business about Sandy's bike came up again and I pointed to the scrubby bit of earth and asked her what plants Sandy was destroying with his bike.

'I planted a tree which cost over twenty quid,' she said. I followed my eyes to the stub at which she was pointing. 'I've spent a small fortune trying to make that little plot nice,' she went on, though I told her that her anger was misdirected and it was Those Kids that were to blame and although she was cross with what they'd done she still referred to them as Lovely Children.

'Lovely children?' I couldn't contain the horror on my face but she stood her ground, as if I had committed some heinous crime.

'People are entitled to have kids and kids are noisy. Kids are here to stay so stop whining and get used to it. The world doesn't revolve around you, you know.'

I had no idea what had given her this jaundiced impression of me but I could feel the storm clouds gathering inside me. 'There is this little thing called consideration,' I retorted, 'a good thing for children to learn, wouldn't you say?' She had no answer to that. Back of the net, I thought. I was in my stride. 'If you don't teach children to consider others, what kind of future does that hold for them, huh? A bunch of inconsiderate people all selfishly doing their own thing and annoying each other...'

I thought that had shut up her for good but oh no. She was ready for more.

'Part of living in a civilised society is tolerance and accepting that nobody is going to change their life to convenience you.'

I was stymied then, I have to confess, because she was full of contradictions. Telling me I needed to be tolerant but then in the same breath saying other people could be inconsiderate and that was fine. More words were said. She sounded like a walking CV at one point when she had to slip in that she was a Nurse and her husband a Social Worker. (She said them with Capital Letters). It was like she was dropping these in not so much to impress as intimidate. (We are professional, middle class people who don't go in for your common and petty neighbourhood disputes, was the subtext.) Like Sandy and I hadn't had any professional training at all! (Sandy used to be big in book reviews and still does freelance work. And me, I once studied homeopathy, which I may have already mentioned). But that really made the O'nions' look small in my opinion. A nurse and a social worker being uncaring about a disabled man's predicament. What hurt most was that I'd always thought of the O'nions' as our kind of people who we could have had round for a civilized chat, or maybe even deeper discussions over caffè latte and amaretto biscuits about the things we see on the news. Like: what do you think about the new Health and Social Care Act? (Not that I'm up to entertaining in the proper sense: cooking meals and the like, because of my Social Anxiety and OCD and the fact that I can't bear other people's mouths on my forks and spoons, especially if they cough or sneeze and what if the meal goes wrong and I'm made to look a fool when other people's meals turn out so well? What if my hand shakes while bringing it in or cutting it or dishing it out? How can I entertain and talk and eat at the same time? These are just a few of my anxieties around that kind of thing. And Sandy is too tired to plan and cook and play host these days and anyway he has a special diet which I'm happy to hide behind as an excuse for not inviting people to meals).

    I don't know why I'm still going along with this pretentious O'nions nonsense anyhow. Didn't Sandy say that the apostrophe was a hypothetical one, to explain the pronunciation? Well, I know my onions and that's all they are. Onions trying to pass as a more wholesome food when in reality they're spoiling the flavour of the dish.

*

Sandy looks at what Carrie's written and tells her to get the rubber. 'It's a good job you wrote it in pencil,' he adds.

'I was thinking of going over it in pen.'

'You can't.'

'Why can't I?'

'You're having me on,' he says. 'You're not serious about including that?'

'Why not?'

He's looking at her like she's lost all sense of judgement.

'You just can't. You can't talk about revenge and feeling victorious and childish name-calling and all these other irrelevancies. And all this stuff about Seroxat Sid loses you credibility.'

She tells him it's true and she's nothing if not truthful.

'You have to be economical with the truth sometimes.'

She asks him if he means she should lie.

'No, not lie exactly. But if say your friend Clo is sensitive about her weight and asks you if you think she's fat, what do you say? The truth?'

She says that's not fair and anyway Clo isn't fat, she may be a bit pear-shaped and she looks bigger than other people only because she's short but she's slimmer than their new neighbour Priss, and it's her diary and she'll write what she likes.

'Well, it started out as a joint journal but now it's become yours.'

She sulks as he switches on the news. 'There's another example,' he says. 'The news. That's a form of truth, isn't it, but it's selected. So it gives a certain impression. But we read between the lines if we're intelligent enough. We don't take it to be the absolute truth. We know there are bits left out, that there are other wars in the world apart from the ones they always report about.'

'Do we? Do we really?' She hates him when he's like this. Having to be right all the time. But the last word is hers. He either has no answer or he can't be bothered with a comeback.

On the Friday, not only does a copy of the report from the sound tests arrive but so does notification of Carrie's DLA award. It is good news. She is still to receive the mobility component at the low rate. It isn't much money but she is so relieved, although her bigger fear, along with Sandy's, is being migrated from Incapacity Benefit to Employment and Support Allowance, the benefit for people who are too ill to work. Down the line there will be more changes coming via Universal Credit, which Carrie and Sandy and their fellow online campaigners have dubbed Universal Chaos. Carrie shelves such distressing thoughts as she picks up the report for the sound tests. The body of the report is five pages long and fleshed out further by all sorts of tables and graphs at the back. Carrie speed-reads the Summary. Something about an assessment of the sound insulation properties of the party wall between No 3 & 4 Pennycott and blah-de-blah the existing structure meets and exceeds the minimum requirements of the Building Regulations blah-de-blah.

She tosses it to Sandy who is more interested in that kind of thing. It doesn't matter anyway. Justine and her baby (plus her husband, if she has one) promise to be model tenants so the results of the report are academic now.

She feels happy as she looks over at a house on a hill from their front bedroom, the furthest one across the counterpane of fields, all lit up by sunshine, while in their back garden the honeysuckle is in flower, the small patches of grass full of clover. Everything in the garden has taken off and gone wild. Next door in Number 4, the paving stones look scrubbed and purged as they wait for Justine and whatever domestic appendages she and her family bring to it to make it their own.

Later, she and Sandy go to the farmer's market in town. They pick up organic meat and home-made lemon cheese and other local produce before travelling over to Looe to stay with Sandy's brother Ken and his wife Dot for the weekend. In the evening they all watch the opening ceremony of the Olympics and on the Saturday they go to the beach at Hannafore. Carrie finds she can do these things if her mental state is willing, though often there is a huge cost in anxiety beforehand. With Sandy there is a huge cost in energy. She understands this because anxiety also depletes the energy. But it is summer and the Tragos have moved out and Quiet Justine will surely have moved in by the time they get home.

Sure enough, on their return, they see evidence of Justine's own stamp, or maybe it is Justine's husband. They see a dog though the trellis, two dogs in fact: a pair of liver-and-white Springer Spaniels, one smaller than the other. Dogs. Justine and her mother kept quiet about that. But the dogs just look with curiosity as Carrie and Sandy pass the house to their front door.

When they're safely inside Sandy says, 'Did you notice the sign on the back door—*Beware the Guard Dogs*—with a picture of a formidable Alsatian above it?'

'Guard dogs? That little one?'

They both snicker. Still, it shows a concern for their property, Carrie supposes. From the back bedroom Carrie sees an inflatable police car full of water and little balls floating around. On the front of it, the letters ELC. Justine looks the kind of mum who would shop at the Early Learning Centre or maybe it was a moving in present from one of her nice young mum friends. Still, the inflatable car's presence, occupying nearly the whole length of the fence, is reassuring to Carrie. The yard now looks child-centred in a pleasing way, instead of a dumping ground as it did before. They hear little noise and are glad to have escaped the inevitable bumps and bangs associated with moving in to a new home.

On the Monday night they watch two programmes about disability benefits. The first, *Dispatches*, features a former GP going undercover to train as a Health Professional for one of the privately funded companies and exposing things like targets for the number of claimants put in the Support Group: the group for the more severely disabled. The woman who is 'training' the undercover reporter explains that with physical assessments, for example, problems with arms, that the disability has to be bilateral (that is, in both arms) to score points. So that if someone has the use of one arm they score no points. The woman says that all they need is the use of one finger which proves they can press a button. The woman herself thinks it is tough but these are the guidelines. Of course, Carrie and Sandy know all this from their campaigning on social media.

The second of the programmes is *Panorama* with the unfortunate title *Disabled Or Faking It?* Carrie and Sandy — and their fellow armchair campaigners — resent this talk of faking, as if somehow there are loads of people out there not deserving of financial help on the grounds of ill health; that, in fact, there are loads of people on the make whereas Carrie and Sandy know that disability benefit fraud is extremely low. But Carrie sees comments posted in disability forums from others supposedly like her: this talk of the genuinely disabled (the people in the forums) and all those who are 'milking the system' (the others) and if it wasn't 'for all those people faking it' out there there'd be enough money to go round. But she and Sandy both know this to be false, suggesting as it does that the amount lost in fraud has to be cut from everyone else's disability benefits to balance the books. She and Sandy both know this isn't the case; they know it is all diversionary tactics. The powers-that-be want to cut back the welfare state anyway, but they need to blame it on the little man or woman, they need to exaggerate it, and they need to divide and rule. It depresses Carrie that she's always having to point these things out to people. Always having to talk about the billions of pounds that go unclaimed from poor and disabled people because they don't know their rights or because pride prevents them from getting their due. As fast as she puts the word out there, misinformation spews back at her tenfold. It feels like a losing battle. It feels like running uphill in sinky mud. She knows it's in the government's interest to have the poor fighting amongst themselves. Classic divide and rule tactics. Which is why both she and Sandy have had to become quite militant. They have to fight trolls on what is sometimes antisocial media. They have to constantly affirm that by spending their disability benefits it is they who are keeping others in employment. They are not passive recipients. Their money is recycled back into the economy. Don't they need food and repairmen and taxis and new laundry? Doesn't their money look the same as a rich person's?

Over the next two or three days, Carrie makes a few more passing observations of her new neighbours in Number 4. In spite of the child's blow-up car in the garden, Carrie hasn't seen an actual car in their parking space which slightly unsettles her: cars give a good indication of when a family is home and when they are out. The Zamoras had the use of two cars, the Tragos had the use of two vehicles as well. A family with no cars hadn't been considered and has Carrie wondering how Justine's husband gets to work. He could walk, she supposes, or get a bus or a lift or a taxi. She's not seen much of Justine's husband, except briefly, getting out of some friend's or relative's car: a tubbyish bloke with mousy hair and a glimpse of builder's bum. He looked twenty-something, same age as Justine.

Carrie got the impression when she met Justine on the sound-testing day that Justine would be out a lot. But today she can hear talking. Conversation through walls sounds tantalizing when you can't quite hear it, like TV programmes with the sound turned down. A man calls round about the boiler—calls at Carrie and Sandy's by mistake—and Carrie directs him next door. That will be why Justine is home, to let in the gas engineer and have her boiler fixed. But the gas man comes and goes and Carrie can still see the child running in and out of the yard. That's another thing, Justine looked the sort of mum to play with her child, to take him out and about, though if Justine is a stay-at-home mum, Carrie's sure she'll do things together with him, not like Mrs Trago and her litter.

Carrie wonders if it's the dogs that are keeping Justine home. You'd think that dogs would get a person out and about more, but maybe that is the husband's duty. After all, it would be a lot having to push a buggy and walk a pair of energetic dogs at the same time.

She's still not seen Justine, except once, from the back, crouching down in the yard, a smile of flesh showing above her jeans as she sprayed weedkiller into the cracks between the paving stones. 'Clueless,' Sandy said. She looked a bit different than Carrie remembers: a bit plumper, but she only met Justine the once and once can be misleading and a bit one-dimensional. Carrie notices the plants in old biscuit tins and flower-pots lining the raised bit in the far corner of the yard, and is at once reassured, just as she was when she saw the Onions' plants. Plants show a homely, tending nature.

Yesterday, when out in the garden she heard the Onions' making a neighbourly approach to Justine. 'If you need anything...' Carrie heard them say. The Onions' sounded very middle-class and civilized. Carrie thinks she should make overtures towards Justine too, now that Justine's no longer her prospective but her actual neighbour, like she and Sandy did with Priss, but she doesn't want to look like she's cribbed the Onions' idea so shelves it for the time being. Anyway, Justine and partner have their own visitors to their new home. Not too many as to be annoying (like the Zamoras) but enough to reassure Carrie that they have a support network and life of their own.

On the Friday, one of these friends comes to visit Justine. From the upstairs window of the back bedroom, Carrie sees the friend sitting in the yard, though it's cool and overcast. Justine is out of view, but she catches shreds of conversation enough to know that Justine's voice has a slight whine to it, like when she talks to her child—is it Noah?—and says, 'when mummy says come here, you come here'.

Sandy calls Carrie away from her watchtower because he says there are more important things to do in the aftermath of *Panorama* and *Dispatches*. Sandy is right of course. There is always work to do, as armchair campaigners. They need to be counteracting the heavy seepage of blame and castigation levelled at disabled and chronically sick people.

Outside in Justine's garden, on the second Thursday in August, and in spite of the warmth, Carrie observes that the deflated police-car paddling pool from the Early Learning Centre has gone, the plants have been torn to shreds and scattered along with the earth over the yard, and the whine of Justine has turned snappy.

In Sainsbury's, the following day, while buying tinned tomatoes and pasta spirals (Sandy insisting on the spirals, though one day Carrie vows to come back with quills or shells, just to test his sense of adventure), Carrie collides with Justine. The moment she sees Justine she knows something is wrong.

'Hi' says Justine, with the friendliest smile.

Carrie knows at once, now that she's seen her again, that this isn't Justine. At least, this *is* Justine, but the girl next door is someone else entirely.

'We decided to buy in the end,' Justine says, almost apologetically. 'We thought we might as well with the amount of rent they were charging.'

And the child in the pushchair is a *girl*. Of course. Carrie remembers now. She queues up with her tin of tomatoes and spiral twists, feeling as deflated as the police car paddling-pool at Number 4. Justine would have been the perfect neighbour, Carrie has no doubt, whereas she has a few reservations about her new neighbours, nothing concrete, just a gut feeling. A sinking feeling.

When she is a few hundred yards away from home with her shopping, Carrie hears someone calling behind her.

'Carolyn?' She turns round to see her other neighbour, Priss, power-walking to catch her up, laden with her own swollen shopping bags. Carrie has only briefly come into contact with Priss since the day she and Sandy first met her, just to wave and smile at, and she's only seen her youngest daughter—aged about fourteen—from afar, and who, now that it's the summer holidays, seems to be out mostly with her mates. This has been a relief for Carrie and Sandy who feared they might be subjected to loud teenage music.

Priss arrives at Carrie's side, out of puff. 'It is Carolyn, isn't it?'

'Carrie.' This is now awkward territory for Carrie. They will have to walk in unison back to their homes, which suddenly feel an impossibly long way off. After their initial bonding, Carrie feels shy again, something which happens if the friendship hasn't had had a chance to cement. It's a bit like going back to square one, having to get past all the formalities again when you've not interacted with an acquaintance for a while.

Priss puts her shopping down as they arrive at the bottom of the ramp leading up to their front doors. 'All that fast walking…am all out of puff now…I shouldn't overdo it, not with my Chronic Fatigue.'

Carrie's not sure whether she should simply carry on up the ramp so she can get into her house quickly, before any more social niceties have to be exchanged, although what she has seen of Priss so far has been nothing but favourable.

Carrie starts up the ramp but can hear Priss close at heel. They stop by their front doors, both searching for their respective keys when Priss says, 'Fancy coming in for a brew? When you've dumped that lot?'

Carrie smiles weakly. She can't summon an excuse quickly enough and so she unpacks her groceries and tells

Sandy where she's going.

'Come on in, hun,' Priss says invitingly when Carrie knocks on the front door, which she notices is on the latch, ready for her. 'I bet you won't recognize the place since you were last here.'

She opens the door to the sitting room. 'Ta-da.'

Carrie makes suitable noises to show she's impressed. The boxes have gone, furniture has been arranged and there's a triptych of those minimalist pictures of flowers above the settee. There are cut roses in a vase on the table and Carrie finds it welcoming. She nods her approval. 'Lovely.'

Priss takes Carrie's order for tea—white, not too strong, no sugar—and disappears to make it. She returns with a mug of tea, far too strong for Carrie's tastes, but Carrie says nothing. She wishes she'd asked for a cold drink now, it being a warm day out.

'So, what are your new neighbours like on the other side, Carrie? I see they have dogs. Springer Spaniels. I'll tell you what, that breed needs a bit of looking after.'

Carrie lifts her mug and blows on her tea, preparing to sip the excessive tannin, to look willing.

'Yes, I thought someone different was moving in—I met them. Well, I met her. She was lovely. Nevermind, I'm sure these will be OK. They can't be worse than the ones before.'

Carrie wishes the last bit hadn't slipped out but there is something about Priss that invites you into her confidence.

'Oh Jesus, no. What were they like then?'

Carrie swallows some of the bitter tea, quickly, so the bitterness won't linger. 'Just…the kids were so unruly…and there were so many of them…I…we…' Priss is hanging on her every word now, twisted round on the settee to face her. 'There was just no peace from them. The pounding, the bumping, and the soundproofing is so bad.'

Priss pats Carrie's knee. 'Oh you poor love. You don't need that. I had the same you know. It was a nightmare. Bloody foreigners they were and all. All their kids dashing about, their noise and mess, spilling into our garden.'

Carrie grits her teeth. It's not just the unpalatable tea but the words too, coming from Priss. She wants to say something. She wants to say, what's their ethnicity got to do with the price of fish? Either people are good neighbours or they're not. Either they're quiet or they're not.

But Priss is being nice to her and Carrie dissolves when people are nice to her. She was never a popular girl at school, she was usually picked last for netball teams, people seemed to befriend her briefly before moving onto someone else. Someone better. She never quite got the hang of long term friendships—until Clo and Sofe.

'You just stick with me, hun.' Priss pats her knee again. 'You just come and let Auntie Priss know if you have any more trouble.'

Priss laughs an infectious laugh, she isn't just physically imposing but something about her character is as well. Carrie laughs with her. She sees a half-completed Sudoku on an occasional table and says, 'not you as well!'

They chat for a while about Sudokus and clothes (Priss notices Carrie's top is in a similar shade of green to her own). 'You and me—we have so much in common, Carrie. I just felt it when we met. You know how you feel when you connect with someone on your first meeting?'

Priss seems to think she has the measure of Carrie. Like they have this pact now. And Carrie's happy to go along with it, all the same.

'How's your work anyway, Carrie? You work in a shop, too, didn't you say?'

Carrie is taken aback by this and quickly blurts out something about the Blue Cross charity shop where she used to work. 'But with all that stuff with the last neighbours—I had to give it up, you know.'

Priss wrinkles her nose in thought. 'I could always see if there's anything going in Morrison's?'

Carrie gasps, shakes her head. 'No, please no! I could never work there. I get terrible panic attacks.'

'Oh tell me about it!' Priss lets out a low guttural laugh. 'We're so alike, you and me!'

Carrie holds her hand to her neck. 'But supermarkets are the worst. I can't even go in them, let alone work in one. I can't really venture much out of the house at all, truth be told.'

'Well, you did OK today, didn't you, hun? It's best to go out and not give in to it.'

Carrie gives a weak smile and wonders if Priss is just incredibly brave or whether her idea of a panic attack is different to Carrie's. Some people say panic attack when they just mean panic, in a flippant sort of way. She doesn't get a chance to ask anyway as the phone rings. Carrie guesses it's Ellie on the other end, the older daughter who's in a wheelchair, and from the way Priss flops down in the armchair and puts her feet on her footstool she looks as if she's in for a long conversation. Carrie mouths her thank-yous and goodbyes and slips out of the front door.

*

Day One

I'm beginning a new journal for the new neighbours. This is the first track as it were. I may not need it, I hope it won't grow into a CD or a double album, but I'm recording this, just in case, because if I don't record, it might be needed later on and I'll be having to rely on memory.

Yesterday, Sunday, August 12th, it was a very warm day and I thought I heard a raised voice or two from next door. Sandy and I went out in the afternoon. We don't normally go out on a Sunday, but since the Tragos have gone and since I've been on Seroxat my symptoms have been more manageable so I stepped into Seroxat Sid and went with Sandy to a café and we sat outside, the weather being glorious. Anyway, I had a milkshake which was really a Barbie-doll-pink liquid with whipped cream on the top. Anyone who knows me knows I don't do whipped cream and Seroxat Sid helped me say something about it to the assistant. 'This is never a milk shake—it just looks like coloured milk.' I pictured Sid's cartoon face as I spoke: a cross between a punk rebel and Desperate Dan, his head huge, his character known to all. But the assistant was not old enough to be a milkshake connoisseur so I stirred the cream in until it did loosely resemble milkshake consistency, though I did still need my shades against the pink glare in my glass.

But the thing is, Mr Vowells (I am assuming it'll still be you who reads this journal if I need to submit it) I didn't want to go *home*. I didn't know why I felt this. It had jack shit to do with the sunshine. Normally (when I used to know what normally was) I would whip home at the speed of light, home being my refuge. But I realized I didn't want to go home because of the raised voices, which reminded me of the Tragos. I can't go through all that again. *You don't have to put up with it.* The words of Seroxat Sid. Or maybe Trish from the Anxiety Group.

Then later, when we got back, we sat in the garden and we heard music—loud music. At first I thought it was coming from somewhere else, but it sounded like it was coming from next door on that side. Number 4 and not Number 2. Priss's car wasn't there anyway. I'd seen her and her youngest daughter, Bethan, loading it up with cases and holiday things in the morning. OK, I thought, maybe it's just because all doors are open on a hot day—that's the problem in summer, doors and windows ajar, polluting the peace—but when I went inside I could still hear it thumping through. For our ears only, and ours alone. I mean, even the Tragos didn't have a full-on, full-up hi-fi. Nowadays it is considered antisocial, much more so than back in the day, when there wasn't the technology, the headphones and suchlike. I started pacing and trying to deep breathe, like they teach you in yoga. Like Fiona Hug-A-Tree from Number 8 whose class I used to attend, once upon. There's something called alternative nostril breathing. 'Sandy, do something,' I said, and then he listed all the strategies:

A) We could do nothing this time—it might be a one-off
B) We could go round and say something (to nip it in the bud)
C) We could post a copy of the Pennycott Resident's Charter through their letterbox which lists loud music as one of the things that disturbs neighbours

'Not A,' I said. 'It's never a one-off and you do have to nip these things in the bud.' He said in that case we should do B or C. 'They should already have a copy of the charter,' I said, having a vague recollection of how your colleague, Mr Hope-Gapp, said in one of his letters or phone calls that he would give future residents a copy of the charter and encourage their involvement in the community.

Then I phoned my friend Sofe who's having similar problems with one of her neighbours and she said it was probably better to go round in person.

So that's what we did, Sandy and me, we opted for strategy B, or rather Sandy and Seroxat Sid did. As usual Sandy pushed me to the forefront. I don't know why he does this when he appears more calm and in control of his emotions, but I think it's to do with me being female. He thinks conflict is less likely to arise where women are involved, even though I was feeling male behind the stubble on Seroxat Sid's papery chin. Sandy was assuming that the guy would answer the door but it was the girl anyway. She looked small, pale, light brown hair tied in a top-knot. Seroxat Sid immediately scarpered and left a rabbit in the headlights, frozen yet wanting to flea off in the direction of her alter-ego. I knew nothing of this girl, who she was, what her reaction would be, but the rabbit stayed there, blinded with fear.

After a few seconds Sandy and I became this double-act: alternating our sentences. We were very polite, just like it says in the handbooks. We couched our complaint in reasonable language so that you wouldn't even know it was a complaint. We prefixed it with a 'sorry to bother you' which always mollifies things, and then I launched into it: 'Sorry to bother you but we can hear your music coming right through our walls.' Sandy then added, 'The soundproofing here is crap.' (The soundproofing card again. Absolving them of blame by shifting the emphasis from unreasonable behaviour to poor structure.) The girl smiled and said she was sorry but 'he' was cleaning upstairs (meaning, we suppose, that they'd cranked the music up so he could hear it upstairs). It was all fairly amicable and afterwards the music was turned down to an acceptable level.

*

Over the next couple of days, Carrie and Sandy don't hear the music but they hear an awful noise of furniture scraping across the slate floor next door, so loud that they can't hear their television or focus on the news.

Carrie is trying to write a blog—under her pseudonym of Seroxat Sid—about work and benefits; about how it isn't work people are afraid of, if they are able to do some, it's the idea of being forced. If work was replaced by the word sex, it would become all too clear to anyone with half a brain cell. Sex being a thing which is freely given, an expression of love or lust between two people. For others, perhaps those who've been in a relationship a long time, the spark may have disappeared and partners may feel it a bit of a tedious duty, like others feel when they've been in their job for too long, but nevertheless, they go through the motions, for other benefits. Those benefits in a marriage or long term relationship, might be security, safety, companionship. The same could be said of work: the job may be stale, but there are benefits such as security, companionship, and of course, there may be financial benefits. Maybe there aren't, maybe the money isn't worth it, just as in the relationship, maybe the job is dead, and time to move on. But none of these cross a line, even if it's only another form of prostitution. At least it is honest. In the same way, forced work, is no different to forced sex. Forced sex has a name. It is rape. If a person doesn't consent to having sex, then it is force.

The raped person feels abused, worthless, guilt,

shame, devalued, angry, powerless. Long term effects may include anxiety attacks, panic attacks, agoraphobia, depression, suicidal thoughts and attempts. Rape is what happened to Clo when she was a teenager, on a one night stand that went badly wrong. Clo didn't tell Carrie this until a considerable time after she'd first met her, until she felt she could trust her. But this is what happens when people lose control of their autonomy, their right to say who they sleep with and when. Everyone knows that in a civilised society this should be a person's right: it gives them dignity, self-worth and self-respect. But then shouldn't this apply to work as well? Work should be a choice: something that also offers dignity, self-worth and self-respect. She and Sandy and all their fellow campaigners have heard all the government rhetoric but on the sly they are using compulsion and force. They aren't the stereotypical rapists who jump at you and overpower you in a dark alley. They are way too clever. They use subtle language, blackmail, power and authority to get you into bed against your will. The results are the same and they are devastating. They take away your autonomy, your ability to act freely, your capacity for choice, your capacity for creativity, your capacity to make a simple decision, your financial independence. In short, they incapacitate you.

Carrie postpones her blog. The furniture noises continue into the evening, invading Carrie and Sandy's living area. Invading Carrie's head. It is the Zamoras' fault. They installed that slate floor. Slate and wood floors may be all the rage but they're cold and noisy and people should think of their neighbours—unless, of course, they don't like them. Carrie remembers being extremely vocal when she heard the drilling and the banging as the slate floor was being installed. The Zamoras must have heard her for Jules Zamora came round with a bottle of red wine as a peace-offering. Carrie was a bit miffed, it gave the Zamoras the upper hand, it was buying the peace, if you like. The subject of the Zamoras' music also came up—it's not too loud for you, is it?—and Sandy said to Jules, 'Well, I'm OK about it, but you like to do your study in the afternoons, don't you, Carrie?' (She was trying to do her correspondence course on the basics of homeopathy at the time, requiring her full concentration). Afterwards, she was furious with Sandy. 'Why did you collude with Jules Zamora against me? Why didn't you have the balls to show a united front against their music?' He had no answer except to say that it was true, that he wasn't as hung-up about their music as she was, but that was only because he wasn't doing home study.

Luckily, she and Sandy are both agreed about the slate floor. It's an awful, amplified noise when pieces of furniture are dragged across it. Carrie is determined to mask the sound by whatever means. Earplugs haven't worked. Not with that sort of impact noise. She's heard that egg boxes are a good shield—recording studios are constructed along this principle, aren't they?—and she even started collecting them once, when the Tragos were there. On recycling days in the town, the greengrocer's and the butcher's had the big cardboard trays that hold thirty eggs but it would have taken loads to cover their party wall and then there was the problem of how to fix them on, not to mention the unsightliness of them.

She phoned companies who advised her on various soundproofing materials and building solutions but she felt bamboozled with the options and sceptical about how effective they would be, not least the expensive ones, and, besides, Sandy needed the money for his MS treatments. It would cost a lot to make their living space a soundproof fortress. She tried the local builders' merchants who recommended a man who came out to look at their party wall and said he'd sorted a similar problem for a woman by fixing foam-backed plasterboard onto her wall. He added that the woman heard noises that other people didn't hear and this rang alarm bells for Carrie. That didn't sound a similar problem to theirs at all. *Everyone* would hear their noises, not just the over-imaginative.

More recently, she and Sandy researched white noise machines on the internet. They found a site and ordered one for £60. It was a drum-shaped object with two speeds, although they didn't differ significantly in tone. Secretly, Carrie was hoping it'd be the answer to all their woes and was dismayed to find that, although it did mask voices, the deeper sounds of bangs and knocks and scrapes still came through. Rather like perfume not quite disguising an underlying body odour.

Carrie doesn't know why she pinned all her hopes on it since it never claimed to be a cure-all.

*

Day Two

The rumbles across the slate floor were really intrusive when we were trying to watch the Channel Four news this evening. I couldn't concentrate on the finer details and neither could Sandy. We want to learn about the wider world but our own narrow world is preventing us from doing so. As well as the TV we had the white noise machine switched on downstairs, which we purchased to the tune of £60. It makes a sound like a rush of wind, though it's quieter than a standard extractor fan, yet we could still hear those deep dragging noises from next door. We asked ourselves whether it was reasonable;

whether we should hear those noises above the TV and the white noise machine? Well, of course it isn't reasonable. We should be able to watch the news in peace (even if there's little that's peaceful in the news these days).

Then we heard the neighbours in the garden, so we decided we should say something over the fence, but as usual we disagreed about who should go. Again, there was this business about it being better coming from a woman. Sandy said he'd go with me, but he was waving his stick around and making heavy weather about getting up, so I kept him in sight in the back doorway to call upon if needed. Just seeing him there, ready to step in, gave me the confidence to broach the subject. But it is a difficult subject to broach, Mr Vowells, because it's not like loud music where it's generally accepted it can be annoying and disturbing to neighbours. And I had to climb up the steps and poke my head through the buddleia branches (which are quite rampant by this stage of August) in order to be seen because the fences are high, although we are glad of this. Good fences make good neighbours, don't they say?

Anyway, the bloke was standing over one side of the garden, the girl right on the other side of our fence which made it difficult for me to look at them both at once, and because I'd spoken to the girl before about the music, I looked at her.

I said, 'Excuse me, but we can hear this awful dragging noise coming through the wall—it sounds like rumbles of thunder.'

The girl looked at me unblinkingly. As she didn't say anything or make it easier for me I carried on. 'You may not me aware—it probably doesn't sound like anything in your house but it's amplified in ours—it's like something being dragged across the floor.' I was faltering and repeating myself. It was the look in the girl's pale eyes, Mr Vowells. I can't describe it but it made me ill at ease. It was an insolent, uncooperative look as if to say, 'Have you quite finished?' Like I was somehow mad for bringing it up.

I should have said, 'I've been here several years—trust me, I know all the sounds.' Or 'Hullo? We were here before you and we'll be here after you've gone?' Trish at the Anxiety Management says 'watch out for that rising or sinking feeling' and this was a sinking feeling moment all right. I knew the girl wasn't going to play ball. Even Mrs Trago sounded as if she would try.

I turned to the bloke because he looked more approachable and open to negotiation: a big bloke, but he didn't look threatening, you might say he was almost cuddly. 'Do you hear the dogs at night?' he said, and I said no because I thought he meant woofing. He asked if it was the tumble-drier and I said no it wasn't that sort of sound, it was like chairs dragging across the slate floor. He did say something about moving the chairs to a new spot but I said 'don't worry' because I felt foolish then that people should have to move their chairs for us but Sandy and I are both adamant that we shouldn't hear these noises and, if anything, we're angry at your colleagues for making us compromise our relationship with our neighbours in this way, especially as you did recommend soft furnishings, and you did hear for yourself how sound transmits when you visited us, even before all the acoustic tests, and the council did have an opportunity to make good the structure between occupancies.

But the thing is the dragging noises have continued, Mr Vowells. Not so much in the evening, but by day, and I thought, to myself, it's *her*. She's doing it to annoy because I had the audacity to mention it. Her brazen expression gave me no confidence. He's out at work during the day, that's why it's been better in the evening. He's taken notice. But they're not in accord. What do you do when they're not in accord? When one neighbour is and the other isn't?

*

During the last week of August, two new wheelie bins are delivered to each household in Pennycott: the black for ordinary household waste; the brown for compost and garden waste. Carrie catches Sandy negotiating with the Onions' over the placement of the new bins.

When he returns to the house Carrie grumbles at him. 'Hullo? Have you forgotten how they were with your bike? On their scrubby bit of earth?' Her miffed tone shouldn't be underestimated. She wants Sandy to stand by her.

'You know I don't do grudges, Carrie. If people are pleasant to me then I don't see why I shouldn't be civil to them in return.'

'A little goodwill goes a long way,' he adds, producing a deep scowl on her face.

'That's my line.'

He grins. 'I know.'

But the truth is she knows he's only this minute remembered it as her line, because she reminded him, and if he can get away with plagiarizing he does. She wouldn't say it was deliberate; more a case of a genuinely unconscious process.

Later, Carrie takes a taxi to Clo's council flat. It's been such a long time since she's been there—so long, in fact, that the settee and other furniture look unfamiliar, but Clo's doing one of those life coaching courses and has been begging Carrie to be a guinea pig for one of her assignments. In all honesty, Carrie can't wait to offload and escape the insufferable atmosphere between herself and the neighbours, one that is also threatening to come between her and Sandy. They are picky and touchy with one another.

When she has settled down at Clo's, tucking her feet under herself on the settee, Clo launches into the session, asking Carrie which area of her life she would like to focus on: an area that might be out of balance with the rest, for instance. Carrie laughs. There's no question which one she will select. 'My Physical Environment, what else?' They both smile and Carrie spends the whole session talking about the Onions', as well as the incident with the girl over the fence in Number 4.

'As you know, me and Sandy spend a lot of time at home so home is important to us.'

Clo nods knowingly, handing the chart to Carrie for her perusal. 'Yes, this one—Physical Environment—has an impact on most of the other areas of my life,' Carrie says, wistfully. 'Health, yes, tell me about it! Romance— what's that?' She gives a wry smile. 'Fun & Hobbies— ditto! Personal Growth—chance would be a fine thing. Sandy makes out that I'm making it worse for myself by listening out for every little knock and bang.'

Clo makes little notes in her beautiful copperplate handwriting.

'OK, I may be a little obsessional by nature, but Sandy is no fan of the noise either.'

Clo continues to listen and take a few notes without judgement, and when she's finished gets Carrie to generate some tasks for the next session involving contacting other housing associations about other possible shared ownership properties and writing to the council about the structural problems.

Later that evening, Carrie drafts a polite letter to the council:

Dear Mr Hope-Gapp
Unfortunately we are again experiencing structure-borne noise eg chairs scraping across the floor, cupboards banging etc. We don't think we should be hearing these noises and we don't think it fair we should be having to compromise our relationship with our neighbours like this.
Please would you give this matter your immediate attention.

Yours sincerely

C & S Cornish

The letter stays on the computer, unprinted.

By the August Bank Holiday, Priss and youngest daughter Bethan are back in situ. Carrie hears Priss outside and hangs about at the top of her steps near the gate, pruning off the browned trumpets on her buddleia, in the hope that Priss will spot her over the fence. Priss is unpegging her washing from her rotary washing line when Carrie calls 'hi'.

Priss turns and waves. 'Fancy a catch up, hun, when I've sorted this lot? I can tell you all about our holiday in Cornwall.'

'Great.' Carrie lays her secateurs down on the top of the raised bedded area. 'I'll come through the back way.'

This somehow feels more intimate, going through Priss's back gate, like they are more than neighbours now. When Edith lived there, she always liked people to use the back gate. Carrie thinks it is good to have Priss back as she descends the steps and through the back door Priss is holding open for her.

'I'll just stick the kettle on.'

Priss returns from the kitchen, and finishes loosely folding the clothes as she removes them from the basket. When she's done, she lowers herself next to Carrie on the settee, phone in hand. She swipes on her phone to show Carrie this picture of the lodge and that picture of the pool, and this one of Ellie in various shots, Bethan in others, all of them together in yet others.

Bethan, who up until now appears to have been lurking, suddenly appears in the sitting room. 'Don't show that one! I look dead fat! I'm on a diet from now on.'

Priss tuts, sneaking a glance at Carrie. 'There's not a pick on her.' Carrie can see this to be true. Then to Bethan she says, 'Wait until you get middle age puff around your face and everywhere else.'

Bethan skulks away from the sitting room with some sort of health drink in her hand. 'Kettle's boiled,' she calls, before pounding off up the stairs.

'She's bored waiting to go back to school,' Priss volunteers. 'These last few days of the summer holidays are always trying.' She lets out a belly laugh. 'There's more of me, so you'd think I'd use up more oxygen. But not when madam's about!'

She rises to sort the drinks. 'Tea?'

In spite of herself and the memories of the bitter tea last time, Carrie tries to give an enthusiastic smile. 'Thanks.' She glances about her and sees a newspaper from a couple of days ago. A *Daily Mail.* She and Sandy and half her Facebook friends call it the Daily Hate Mail or worse. They all hate it. As they do *The Sun,* which they dub The Scum and *The Daily Express* which Carrie has dubbed The Daily Ex Lax. Whenever Carrie or Sandy see one in a public place, such as the dentist's waiting room, they will shudder. They will make loud huffing and puffing noises. Seroxat Sid will do more. He will let out an exasperated shriek, and say something along the lines of 'eeyuk, I can't bear to breathe the same air as it,' amid strange and disconcerted stares, or embarrassed shakes of said newspaper from the Mail faithful.

Priss arranges the coaster on the occasional table beside Carrie and places her mug of tea there, which looks as dark as last time. With her foot, Priss nudges another small table over to her side and places her own drink there. There's a chip in Priss's cup. Carrie didn't expect chips in Priss's cup. There are also chips in her nail polish. There is perhaps something more fractured about Priss than Carrie realized.

She seems to be looking at Carrie with probing eyes and a twisty grin. 'So how's it been with your other neighbours, hun?' Priss nudges her head to the right, in the direction of Number 4. 'Any trouble?'

Carrie screws her face up; she feels she can't conceal anything from the penetrating eyes. 'A bit noisy.'

'Oh no! What, like loud music and stuff?'

'There's been a bit. And raised voices and lots of banging and clattering around.'

Priss nods knowingly. 'Do they work? I bet they don't. They'll be one of those families popping kids out and expecting the state to pick up the tab out of my taxes.'

Carrie's features become rigid with shock. 'They only have one child,' she says, non-plussed that she should be defending her latest neighbours in Number 4. 'Anyway, benefit payments aren't a one-way street. Claimants spend money too. They buy food and fuel and trips in taxis. They pay VAT and—'

'Oh Carrie, hun. We can't afford it. There's so many

of those people bleeding this country dry.'

Carrie smiles to hide her mounting anger. 'Oh, what, the bankers and Chief Executives, you mean? I agree. We're the sixth richest nation in the world but most of it is being spent on the cost of appeals so people can get what they're entitled to.'

'Oh don't start me on the culture of entitlement.' But Priss isn't really listening to Carrie, she's only absorbed in her own little rant. 'I lived next door myself to a family who had just that sense of entitlement, before we moved here. Nightmare they were.' She leans forward and mouths 'immigrants on benefits' in a conspiratorial fashion, like Carrie will agree with her and change all her views at the mention of immigration.

Carrie feels her stomach roiling. Surely this is a wind up. But Priss's expression says otherwise. Carrie doesn't know where to begin. She likes Priss, or thought she did, but not the words filing out of her mouth. It'll be *The Daily Mail.* Filling her head with it all. She opens her mouth then, trying to locate the words of protest tumbling over one another in her brain.

'He works, the guy in Number 4…and actually Sandy is on benefits, you know…'

Priss peers over her cup mid-sip. 'Oh that's different. He's genuinely disabled. Like my Ellie– '

'Genuinely?' God how she hates that word. She knows what's coming next, like she wrote the script.

'Well, you know. There's all these people faking it, aren't there, irregardless of the spiralling welfare costs.'

Carrie frowns and hopes her look of disgust and dismissal is plain for Priss to see. 'No, hardly any actually. Less than one per cent. That's pretty low in my books!'

'Yes, but they are making it worse for the genuine people, like my Ellie. Like your Sandy.'

'Like me.'

Carrie wishes she could retract her last words because Priss is ogling her now.

'You? There's nothing wrong with you, is there?'

'Not all disabilities are visible, you know. Especially mental health ones...I find it hard to go out of—'

'Oh I know there's people with schizophrenia, hun. People in hospital and the like. Of course those people should be helped. But panic attacks? I mean we all get them from time to time but we have to soldier on. We can't all crumple because of a panic attack, Jesus!' Before Carrie has a chance to ask her if she knows how debilitating a panic attack can be, Priss is already reaching for her *Daily Mail*. 'There's something in this most days about people taking the piss...where is it now...some guy who claimed thousands of disability benefits claiming he needed a walking stick but was able to play football perfectly well.'

Carrie wonders if Priss is expecting her to go along with it. Maybe she is surprised to And didn't she once tell Priss she suffered with panic attacks? 'Those right-wing papers are pure bile, you know, all full of poverty porn...they set poor against poor and distract us from the real facts, from the real fraudsters at the top.' She is getting into her stride now, she feels confident from all the arguments she's had on Facebook and social media. She can trot out the lines and counterarguments with the best of them. 'You want to try reading *The Guardian* or *The Huffington Post* or *The New Statesman*.'

'What, you mean Leftie papers?'

'Ones that will give you the other side.'

Priss gives the twisty grin and a little snort. 'Oh I don't like many of those Tories toffs either, hun. Only Nigel Farage can sort this country out.' Then her eyes become stirred up with an intensity which Carrie sees is hostility. Not to her specifically, but to some imagined enemy. 'But I mean I have always worked, even when the kids were small. But why should I when I can get more on benefits?'

Carrie feels herself juddering. 'Benefits have been slashed and there are more cuts on the way.'

'Good.' Priss is getting fired up as much as Carrie. 'There are some that have been taking the piss for far too long.'

Carrie closes her eyes. Breathes out shakily. 'Tell me, Priss. why would you want to be on benefits anyway? If you believe that work is such a noble thing? Surely you're where you want to be?'

Priss puffs, shaking her head. 'No, we have to work and pay our taxes, m'deario. It doesn't mean we like what we do.'

'But why shouldn't we do something that we enjoy?'

Priss is regarding her now with something akin to disbelief. 'Are you for real?' She gives an exasperated shake of her head. 'We can't all be job snobs. How else are we going to pay for the NHS and our schools if we all had that attitude?'

Carrie wants to reply but there are too many retorts flying through her head at once so that she's unable to settle on one. The tension remains in the air, even though Priss has changed the subject back to the other neighbours and the little child and the dogs. But their tenuous friendship is now another fractured thing, Carrie knows, as she stands to go and, rather curtly, thanks Priss for the tea before letting herself out. It was a mistake to talk politics and benefits, to allow herself to be dragged into it, although Sandy, and Clo and Sofe, and her online friends would congratulate her for doing so.

She realizes by the time she gets through her own back gate, down the steps and through the back door, she is stomping.

'Sandy, I've said too much to Priss.' She hurls herself down beside him. 'About us being on benefits.'

She's waiting for him to say, why on earth did you do that, but he just says, 'So? It's nothing to be ashamed of. We are entitled to them. We've done nothing wrong by being ill.'

'I know…of course we haven't. But it's the climate.'

Sandy shakes his head. 'Holy shit balls! Do you remember when it was the climate to moonlight and nobody batted an eyelid? When you just told your employer you had to nip out to sign on.'

Carrie just about remembers, although it all seems so dim and distant. 'I suppose I thought Priss would understand, having a disabled daughter and everything. But I should have known that some of our own can be the worst. She's like so many people. She understands what she can see, physical disability, like yours, but even then she came out with the classic lines…pointed to an article in the Daily Hate about someone cheating the system.'

Sandy snickers. 'Hope you told her what for!'

'Oh I did that all right.'

Sandy reaches an arm around the back of her and gives her shoulder a squeeze. 'That's my girl.'

Tears of fury are spilling out now. 'And...and she dismissed panic attacks.'

'Well, people who don't get them...they can't be expected to understand—'

'Oh no! She gets them...she just soldiers on!'

Sandy throws his head back and a fully fledged laugh escapes this time. 'Martyrs. The worst kind.'

'She's a Kipper an' all. Thinks the sun shines out of Nigel Farage's backside.' Carrie wipes her tears with her sleeve. 'And I wish she'd bloody stop calling me 'hun'. Why does everyone do that nowadays?'

She manages a snuffly snigger in anticipation of Sandy's reaction to her next complaint. 'And she came out with your number one bête-noire!'

Sandy titters. 'Not *irregardless?* She never did!'

Carrie nods, 'She did, really.'

They both have a secret sneer at this, it feels good for a fleeting second. But Carrie thought she'd found a neighbourhood ally in Priss, someone she could rely on, somewhere to go when the noise got too much. But Priss is another who cannot be entirely trusted and Carrie knows she and Sandy must tough it out alone. Thank goodness they have each other and an online community out there.

*

Days Three To Five

These early September days can be very warm, Mr Vowells, and at lunchtime the other day, when passing the neighbours' place in Number 4, I noticed that the dogs were left alone in the yard and had finished their water. There were two white plastic bowls, which had probably been filled, but they weren't proper dog bowls, they were daft-shaped, all narrow at the bottom, like the sort you would beat eggs in, the kind that dogs would have over in no time. This is exactly what happened to one of the bowls. Sandy and I couldn't get access to the yard, it was padlocked from the inside, so we had to aim our watering can over the fence at the back so that the water landed in one of these plastic bowls and boy, the dogs lapped it up, you should have seen them. Of course, the smaller dog, Pepper, tipped it up again eventually, so later on we put some more water in an old butter tub on the step so that they could reach it through the gaps in the trellis. Pepper went for all the water in the tub but the bigger dog, Paddy, wasn't getting any and barked in frustration because he couldn't get his larger head through the trellis. They don't understand turn-taking, you see. So I decided to get the watering can again and aim for the plastic bowl in the yard, which wasn't so easily reachable in its new position but we managed it so Paddy could have some water. All in all, the dogs were left out from morning until 7pm when their owners returned. It was a pretty hot day and their water ran out at lunchtime (possibly earlier) and there is very little shade in their yard.

A couple of days after it was another warm sunny day (Day 4) and the dogs were locked out again but I couldn't see *any* water this time when I looked out of our window at lunchtime. Maybe the dogs had ran out of water, but it meant we had to put water over the fence again. We couldn't reach their vessels with the watering can this time so we found a small plastic bucket under our sink and tied garden twine round each end of the thin metal handle, filled it with fresh tap water and lowered it over the fence. The dogs lapped up the water and fought over it, poor things.

We then put a note through next door saying, YOUR DOGS RAN OUT OF WATER AGAIN SO WE HAD TO GIVE THEM SOME OVER THE FENCE. DOGS NEED A LOT TO DRINK IN THIS WEATHER. Both my friends Clo and Sofe said that I should have called the RSPCA but I'm always one for giving the benefit of the doubt. Too nice for my own good, my dad says. But I thought maybe it really was just ignorance and the note would alert them for the future. Sofe says that Springer Spaniels also need lots of stimulation but all they've got is this grubby twist of old rope, an end of which they each grit between their teeth in a friendly tug-of-war (in the cooler weather, at any rate). In this weather they just flop out on the sizzled concrete, Pepper's head nestled on Paddy's bigger, older body. Now you may be thinking that this isn't your department, Mr Vowells, that it's of more interest to the animal welfare people, but there's also been excrement over the yard for the past few days, making it unpleasant to sit in our garden because of the smell and the flies. We've tried lighting incense but we could still smell wafts of it and were forced to retreat indoors. This, we understand, is very much your domain, Mr Vowells, and I feel we may have to contact you or Mr Hope-Gapp soon in relation to this matter because this situation cannot continue unchecked.

The neighbours' response to our note about the dog water problem was to keep their dogs indoors. I can't say I understand such a response. Most dog-lovers would have been horrified. They'd have knocked on neighbouring doors with anxious expressions until they'd found the public-spirited folk who'd written the note. They'd have said, 'Oh thank you for giving our dogs water. We'd no idea they'd run out.' But then reasonable people wouldn't have left their poor dogs languishing in a hot concrete yard with insufficient water in the first place. I will say that since the note we have seen this spanking new water contraption looking very incongruous in the fouled-up yard. (Day 5). It's like one of those that Sofe told me about where it's difficult for the water to run out or get tipped up because with every uptake of water, more comes down to fill its place.

But the point of these entries is not about the dogs' liquid requirements in hot weather. It's more about their exercise requirements and the fact that they're not getting walked, which means they have bursts of frenetic activity at any time of the day or night. This sleep deprivation is taking its toll on my mental health.

*

The following day, Carrie notices her neighbours in Number 4 have acquired a car. A red Montego. This is a hopeful sign. A car will give them mobility; will hopefully take the girl, the child and possibly the dogs away from the house as much as possible. Carrie is getting claustrophobic with them home so much. To think when she lived with Iain all those years ago she used to long for neighbours to be home; couldn't bear to think of them all out enjoying themselves. It unsettled her if all the houses around them were empty on a Saturday night. Lights on but no-one home. 'We're missing out, Iain,' she used to say, until he had enough of missing out on his true sexuality and far-off lands, like Goa.

A couple of days later and an old friend of Sandy's phones to say he will be passing through on his way to Cornwall, around four o'clock give or take, and Carrie reserves their parking space by putting a traffic cone in it. She acquired this cone several years ago after the Zamoras had got upset when her parents parked in the Zamoras' space. Carrie had noticed the nearby roadworks and the plentiful cones—big jumbo ones—and set about stuffing one in a black refuse sack one night, carrying her swag home under the cover of darkness. When she told her dad he said she had a touch of the anarchist about her. She liked that. It's true, she does.

She places the cone towards the back of the space for Sandy's friend, rather than in the middle. She does this so that the friend—Brian—won't have to leave his car to move the cone back but can drive straight into the space, nudging the cone back with his bumper, if needs be. At the same time the presence of the cone in the space is to alert other opportunists that the space is reserved.

At three o'clock, Carrie notices that someone else has

parked in their neighbours' space and at around half past three she sees the neighbours' red Montego return. They are hovering near her space but they can't park there, they wouldn't dare, not with the cone there. But these neighbours are different than most people it seems. They operate by a different set of codes for they are backing into Carrie and Sandy's reserved parking space.

Carrie knows there's a rational adult inside her somewhere, fighting to get out. She has occasional fantasies about being reasonable with the new neighbours, where they all discuss things amicably and see one another's point of view and all go off to one another's houses where the kettle is on. But this isn't one of those occasions. Seroxat Sid whooshes into her skin and marches her feet out of the back gate in high dudgeon. *How dare they park there!*

'Excuse me, you're in our parking space!' Seroxat Sid is keeping her pumped up as the words fly out to the light-eyed, pale-faced girl who is just opening the car door on the nearside.

'Well there's someone in ours.' (Not: Oh I *am* sorry). Naturally, the defensive little retort doesn't go down well with Carrie. 'Hullo? What d'you think the cone's there for? Decoration?'

At this stage, any reasonable person would vacate the space, having realized their error, but the bloke who up until now Carrie's had down as the more reasonable voice of the partnership pipes up in an offhand tone, 'We only want it for fifteen minutes.'

Carrie turns her back on them, waves her hand in the air and stomps off in defeat—wishing she could have kept Sid in her head a little bit longer.

Sandy doesn't help matters by telling her she should have held out.

'Pfff. It's easy for you to say from the safety of your armchair!' It's true. He's happy for her to go that extra distance where cars and territory are concerned, especially if she's the one having to do it, but the truth is she yielded for the sake of her anxiety state; to prevent it slipping into a full-blown 'episode'.

'War usually begins small,' Sandy says, after a report on the news of the continuing conflict in Syria; of more shellings, more deaths. 'Inside us. In communities like these. A microcosm right here at Pennycott. Then it spreads to nations.'

She ignores what she sees as him taking the moral high ground. She takes the remote from him and switches channels. He accuses her of monopolizing the remote, adding, 'It's not called a remote control for nothing. You control it!'

*

Day Six

Think of each one of the days that I record incidents as equivalent to four or five unrecorded days, Mr Vowells, and that the days that I do record are a culmination of several similar incidents. If you think of it this way, Mr Vowells, you'll be nearer to the extent of the problems we face.

Yesterday there was lots of crashing around and shouting for half an hour or so around lunchtime. We were out earlier so it may have been going on longer but I felt so on edge I had to escape to Sofe's place, a few roads away in Dart Close. She has problems with a neighbour too—a man who blares his music enough to make her wall vibrate and when she says anything he turns his music up even more—so she understands what I'm going through. But sometimes I just want to close the door on our house and never come back. I just want to keep on walking and wish I could be one of these people who just takes off with a sleeping bag and the clothes they stand up in and sleep in a field under the stars. Sid would do that. He would bum a lift and see where life takes him.

But instead, as I write this today, I am ill in bed with a stomach bug. I'll spare you the details but for the last few nights I've heard that awful scraping noise across the kitchen floor. Sometimes it's been at bedtime and last night it woke me up at 2.30 am and then again around 6 am. We know it's the dogs now because at bedtime last night, when Sandy heard all that scraping, he stepped out into the garden and saw that all the lights were off next door, as if they'd all gone to bed, so it can only have been the dogs. Now it makes sense to me why the guy said to me over the fence that time, 'Is it the dogs you can hear?'

My friend Sofe says Springer Spaniels are hyper and she wouldn't want one. She's been the owner of several dogs in her time. She has a greyhound at the moment, as they're quiet, delicate dogs. She says the police train Springers to sniff out drugs and they use them in prisons for the same purpose.

But the point is, Mr Vowells, I drafted a letter to your colleague Mr Hope-Gapp because we pussyfooted around too long with the last neighbours, the Tragos, when really this is either a soundproofing problem or it's a noise problem. If it's a soundproofing problem then your colleagues should be implementing those recommendations of yours and fitting the place out with soft furnishings and proper sound insulation. But if it's a noise problem then the tenants should be warned that their actions may result in a noise abatement notice or whatever it is you issue them with. Not that you can serve noise abatement notices on dogs. Dogs will be dogs. But you can blame their owners for not walking the beasts. Actually, they're not beasts at all. They're really rather lovely animals and I do feel sorry for them. Both Clo and Sofe say dogs need a lot of walking, especially this breed. But it occurs to me that our neighbours have never kept dogs before. They perhaps fancied the idea when they got the house. That's why their pot plants got torn to shreds, for anyone who'd owned dogs before would have surely known that.

But today I am ill in bed and I can't even sleep off the bug because of all that clatter. I've tried earplugs. But I can hear so much knocking on wood. Every sound echoes like a drum. Someone had some fireworks the other night, and the popping and banging sounds they make are not dissimilar to what we hear on a daily basis. Today, I had to knock on the wall but if anything the clattering increased. Or it didn't subside at any rate. I think it may be the girl cleaning. She probably has to clear up after the dogs and hoover up all the dog hairs. It sounds like a hoover attachment against the stairs. I can hear her shouting at her kid every so often. 'Stop it!' or 'Get down, Noah!' Sometimes I hear her shouting at the dogs to get out and I get the feeling I'm hearing a neighbour who is not happy keeping quiet. I can hear her music faintly playing as she cleans. It's a resentful rather than a respectful quiet—one that puts me on edge. It's like she really wants to be playing her music loud and I'm cramping her style. But she can't play it loud so she should learn to live with it or, should I say, without it. We'd all like to play our music loud. I've stood where she is, dying to do what I please when I please. Now I'm standing on this side, yearning for peace and quiet. Trying to be considerate. It's all I can do not to stoop to her level. Tit for tat. But I've done that with the Zamoras. It's like I want to say to her, 'I can do quiet cupboards or I can do loud cupboards, know what I mean?' And my, does she do loud cupboards. The slams are just as distressing as the bass beats on a hi-fi. More, they are sudden and unpredictable.

*

When Carrie checks in for her next appointment with Trish at the local Mental Health Team, she feels already riled. The receptionist doesn't help by waiting a considerable time before buzzing through to Trish to inform her of Carrie's arrival, giving the impression that Carrie is late and a come-day go-day person who can't be bothered turning up for appointments on time. But it's a standard joke between Carrie and her friends that on the rare occasions when she's had to travel somewhere important—in the days when she still had engagements—she would arrive so early she would be in time for the earlier train.

Luckily, Trish knows Carrie a bit better. Or so she hopes. But Carrie thinks even Trish has failed to get a handle on the full extent of her anxieties and OCD, otherwise she wouldn't come out with things like, 'How would your life be if you didn't have this situation with the neighbours?' This is when her anxiety can inflame into anger. It must be a trick question for surely the only possible answer is 'wonderful'. Trish maybe thinks she's being clever with such a question, as if somehow Carrie hasn't *thought* what it would be like or as if she might confess to her life being empty or that she somehow needs these difficulties with the neighbours. The question, in some deeply psychoanalytic sense, whiffs of smugness. Like—I bet you hadn't looked at it this way,

Carrie, and your silence, your pondering on your reply is confirmation of this because I've stunned you, have I not, with this revelation. Whereas Carrie's silence is only a non-response at being asked such an oblique question. Such a *dumb* question. She knows she wouldn't be here at all if people looked on her condition as physical, like Sandy's, instead of psychological. The fact that it is named (and shamed) as psychological means that you get people like Trish with their theories and tricks and misplaced sympathies, and she's supposed to lap them up, be grateful, because most people *aren't* sympathetic in the way they are about arthritis or MS—Priss was a case in point—even though some physically disabled people are able to do more than she can, like drive a car. That's why she tries to talk in symptoms. Fast heart beat *is* physical. As is dizziness. As is a headache, gut ache, IBS, sweating, trembling and nausea. If only there was another name instead of phobia. Or panic. Or OCD. Or neurosis. They will find out all these things are physical in the end, she's no doubt of that. All down to some dodgy neural transmitter. Or a weakness in the nervous system, and they'll come up with a name to match. A name that takes it seriously so that you won't end up in the clutches of Trish and her What would your life be like if—?

In spite of herself, Carrie keeps her mind focussed on the neighbour situation. 'There's no mileage,' she says, 'thinking about what-ifs and might-be's. This is the situation I'm in and I want to know what's the best way to deal with it.'

She goes on: 'I mean, she can battle with me all she likes, this neighbour, but she won't win.'

A conversation about Conflict Resolution emerges, to which Carrie responds by saying, 'In my experience these things are never fully resolved. At best, they're only resolved till next time,' and she's glad to have temporarily stymied Trish which is not that easy a thing to do. But it's true, this is her experience, and Trish is now interested in past conflicts in Carrie's life. Is this a pattern? It certainly is not, she's able to state this quite emphatically for she knows where Trish is trying to go with this. But the truth is she never used to be in conflict with anyone. She got on with everyone, so much so that a boy she wanted to dump at the age of sixteen she was still saddled with at eighteen for fear of hurting his feelings. And when she went to work (during those short phases where she sampled nine-to-five employment) she'd come home with an aching mouth on account of laughing at unfunny jokes and a wish to please. Yes, she was a people-pleaser. She wasted too much of her life this way instead of sometimes being a self-pleaser. But somewhere, somehow, over the years, there's been a transmogrification. People started falling out with her, people she'd known for years, and she could only put it down to the fact that she was now standing up for herself and what she believed in and didn't suffer fools gladly. Isn't this why she pissed off Priss? And isn't this why Priss has avoided her ever since? Yet an admittance of this aloud, and Trish will seize upon it and have it all labelled as a pattern of behaving, her issue, her problem, her overreaction, instead of the perpetrators'—that is, the neighbours. So Carrie keeps schtum.

    She supposes this business with the neighbours all started when they had the Zamoras on one side, and Edith on the other who they had to consider. They had to reconcile the two different lifestyles on either side and come up with a solution, a compromise. When she thinks about the Zamoras now, she would welcome them back with open arms for all their foibles. *His* heavy-footed presence—a strong footfall suggesting confidence and manliness or maybe just compensating for his smallness and his stoop. And *her* endless capacity for socializing and trying to keep up with her globe-trotting friends, up half the night listening to music, always laughing, anything but be a party-pooper.

But what *is* she thinking—she would welcome them back with arms outstretched, indeed. It's all their fault for selling the house next door to the council in the first place. It's all their fault for putting in the slate and laminate flooring.

*

Day Seven

I didn't want to be recording loads of tracks, but we have half a new CD already.

Sandy and I returned from my parents tonight before seven, having been away for a long weekend. I can't tell you how I wanted to stay on there, walking down by the stream with my mum, while Sandy chewed the fat with my dad. My mum and I stood on the small bridge, in silence, enjoying the birdsong and the soothing sound of rushing water. An odd dipper or wagtail to enthrall us. Wondering if the kingfisher might put in a rare appearance. But I stood there, trying to absorb that peace and calm into my being—take a little piece away with me, to call on in times of need. But it's difficult to keep hold of that magic when you're travelling home on a noisy train and by the time you're home it's all but dissipated. When you've been away, all you want to do is sink back into your house, your quiet house, and put your feet up.

But around 7.30 pm we heard bangs and knocks and scrapes for about fifteen minutes, right up until the break in Coronation Street. I said to Sandy it sounds like footsteps, but when I put my ear to the wall I realized it was dog paws and I could hear howling. We soon learnt that one of the dogs was indoors, the other outdoors. A couple of hours later and the dogs were woofing incessantly. The one outside was woofing at the one inside. The one inside howled at the one outside. They sounded very distressed and frustrated because they could hear but couldn't see or reach one another. But what sort of pea brain does it take to do that? What good would separating the dogs do if they're still within earshot? It was always going to cause upset, wasn't it? For dogs and neighbours. I suppose our neighbours had this ill-thought out idea that separating them would stop them getting up to mischief and goading each other.

I wondered out after ten o'clock to see whether any other neighbours were being disturbed by the barking and sure enough there was our other neighbour, Rick Onions, walking round to Number 4. For a moment I forgot all hostilities with him; right now I needed him as my ally.

I said to him, 'Are you hearing what we're hearing?' Then I added, 'There's no one in. They've left one dog inside and one dog outside.'

We stood in the darkened alley outside Number 4. I looked into his squidgy eyes but they weren't smiling at me.

'I've got no time for antisocial behaviour,' he said. 'My wife's trying to sleep. She's got an early shift tomorrow.'

For a split second we connected, but tomorrow we wouldn't speak of it, I knew. We would go back to passing in the street with heads bowed. But he called it Antisocial Behaviour, all that woofing, and that was enough for me. No grey areas, Mr Vowells. I realized then that's how other people view it. As ASB. Sandy and

I have pussyfooted about too long with this, and it's time we also wrote to your colleague Mr Hope-Gapp who, as landlord, has powers.

Day Eight

I must mention the dog fouling in the yard, which hasn't been cleared up for days. As you can imagine, two dogs, none of whom is getting walked and whose only lavatory is the back yard, are bound to produce a considerable amount of waste. It's dotted all over the yard in squirls and squiggles—I took a couple of photos from the back bedroom this morning, Mr Vowells, which is evidence, although I wish there was something that records smells. All that poo makes sitting in our garden a most unpleasant affair, requiring endless incense to make it remotely bearable. The incense is making the insects go a bit potty.

I remember the garden when the Zamoras lived there—there were plants in ceramic tubs, and in the raised area in the corner they used to stick night-lights in tall candle-holders when they were socializing with their well-travelled circle. Though loud, the conversation was at least high-spirited and aspirational. Come to think of it, it was the Zamoras who covered over the grass with paving slabs, making it into a patio. Now, you wouldn't dare call it a patio. It's a soiled yard with bits of old rubbish collecting at the edges. It looks like a down-at-heel council property rather than an aspirational shared-ownership home. The Onions' must be able to smell it.

There are flies from the dog crap, Mr Vowells. We have to keep our living-room door closed on these warm September days, even though September is one of my favourite months, when the sun is mellow but still warm, and it's costing me a small fortune in fruit because I can't eat the fruit from our fruit bowl in case a toxicara-infested fly has touched it, and if a fly lands on my plate I have to chuck the whole plate out because it puts me off using that plate forever, no matter how much scalding water or Fairy Liquid is applied to it, because of my OCD. I know you'll see my point of view, because health is your business, Mr Vowells. And I can't sit in the living-room until I have beaten every last wayward fly to a pulp, or sent it reeling in stunned surprise back from whence it came with a swift thwack of *The Guardian*. And I couldn't even attempt today's Sudoku, even though Sandy removed the splatted entrails of the fly (its blood red like mine) to copy out a grid for me, so he duly completed it himself. It's not as if killing comes naturally to me. I hate harming any of God's creatures. I am a pacifist, I think you realize that by now. But I loathe the thought of disease even more, as I know you do. Why else would you have chosen to work in this field?

I mention God, though I'm really an agnostic kind of gal, a kind of lapsed Pagan, if you will, if there can be such a thing, but I'm beginning to think that even prayer would be more effective than writing this log. Trouble is, I call on God's services so infrequently that I don't expect any immediate results there either. Praying is probably a skill or an art like any other and probably requires persistence, though when you think about it, I have taken up so little of the Almighty's time that he surely owes me. You owe us too. So have no doubt, we will be contacting you or one of your colleagues about this matter in the near future.

*

In fact, Carrie bashes out a letter later to Mr Hope-Gapp

the following day after another sleepless night.

She mentions the noise and the stench. The dogs going berserk at nights after being shut indoors all day, except during the very warm weather when they were kept out all day. She writes about the smell of dog do and all the flies it attracts and how the horrible stink puts her and Sandy off sitting in their garden. She mentions how the dogs bark from distress or being shut in all day.

She summarises the adverse effects it's all having on their health and how she has had to increase her medication.

Carrie is pleased with the letter as she prints it off and pops it in a brown envelope.

But, after almost a week, she gets herself into an inflamed state as a result of the council's non-response to her letter. She's beginning to doubt her signature and wondered if she signed it Seroxat Sid by mistake. She begins pacing (always a bad sign), and swearing she will give those ignorant eejits what for. But Sandy tells her no. He tells her it is far more effective to do ultra-polite (rather than vitriolic) along the lines of: 'I realize you must be very busy but if you would spare a few moments to address my concerns I'd be most grateful.' The laid-on-thick-with-a-trowel won't be lost according to Sandy, though Carrie says it sounds sarcastic and it would get *her* back up.

Just as they are discussing it there is a knock on her front door. Through the spyhole Carrie sees who it is. She turns to Sandy through in the lounge and mouths 'Priss'. He shrugs. 'Well aren't you going to answer it?' He doesn't seem to be as fazed as she is. She sees Priss's head rendered top-heavy by the spyhole, her eyes lowered, her head looking to the side. Then she takes a step backwards, appearing to look up at the front bedroom. She's looking reasonable enough, Carrie observes. Perhaps she should overlook it this time, the feelings she felt when Priss came out with all that stuff about benefits last time—and before she knows it, she has opened the door.

Priss sways her head to the side, eyes on Carrie. 'Hi! Only me! Can I have a quick word?'

'Sure…come in.'

It occurs to Carrie that Priss has never set foot in her house before. She is unsure whether to carry on the conversation in their dark and narrow hall or to invite Priss in properly. Sandy is calling 'hi' and 'come on through' anyway. They exchange social niceties while Carrie offers drinks and gets the kettle on. She feels they and their house are under scrutiny, even though Priss seems friendly enough. Carrie sees Sandy's toenails need clipping—poking through his sandalled feet beneath his jogging bottoms—she usually does them for him, but it's only the presence of visitors that draws her attention to such things. Especially smartish people like Priss.

'Take a seat,' Sandy tells Priss, rising slowly with the aid of his stick—the funky one with the white spots on black—to clear a space for her on the settee. Priss smiles and parks herself at the far end, assisting Sandy with the tidying up of the old newspapers and flyers that have made way for her backside.

She settles herself down, brushes the lapels of her jacket and looks over the side of the settee.

'Oh is that one of those money plants?' She leans over and feels the leaves. 'There's some new roots growing off this bit…can I take a cutting? I could do with some money!'

'Sure. The plants are Carrie's but I'm sure she won't object.'

'Great. Thanks.' Priss nips a promising bit off the plant without too much effort and, at Sandy's invitation, breaks off another loose sprig to stow away with the first in her handbag.

Then she straightens her blouse and sits forward. 'What I came round to say was...' She does a little cough into her fist. 'That dog mess next door to you. It's awful.' Carrie fetches in the drinks, finding a coaster for Priss. 'I can smell it every time I go up the steps to my car. I will back you up with whatever action you decide to take. We shouldn't have to put up with it.'

Sandy smiles and nods. 'Thanks. A bit of moral support is always good.' He picks up the mug of steaming tea Carrie's placed beside him, takes a sip. 'Carrie's written to the guy at the council. In fact we were just discussing their lack of response but if you contact them as well, that may make them act more quickly...they like corroboration.'

'No problem.' Priss pulls her skirt towards her plump knees. 'I saw in a TV listings magazine that an independent film company are looking for people in the south west, you know, to take part in a neighbours-from-hell-type documentary. They have one of the major channels interested. I thought they—' she says, butting her head towards Number 4, 'I thought they might qualify. I saw all that dog shit through their trellis and so I phoned up the film company person on impulse and left my phone number after the recorded message! Nobody's got back to me yet.' There's a look of disdain in her eyes and her smile fades out. 'It's not on, though.'

'Go for it,' Sandy says, while Carrie perches herself on the cane chair, mug of tea in her hands. They now have an ally in Priss, who it would be as well to keep onside. Their previous clash of views on benefits and newspapers, during an innocent social call, has made Carrie question whether she should live and breathe her politics to the extent that she does, proudly and loudly, or whether she should compromise. Or, indeed, shut it away in a cupboard altogether beneath polite coasters and safe civil smiles over a hot mug of something, for the sake of friendship. For the sake of peace.

*

Holiday Log

Sandy's brother Ken and his wife Dot—hearing all our problems—invited us for a break with them in Looe. I was so determined to go, so determined not to be ill before going away, I had to put my life even more on hold than usual, turning down Clo's offer do a life coaching follow-up session with me. I've really not been able to put my mind to it and Clo sounded distinctly nasal prompting a response from me along the lines of: 'You haven't got a cold, have you?' said in such a way that meant not so much 'Poor you, Clo' as 'Don't come round, I don't want to get it.' I didn't mean for it to sound like that but then Clo understands my germ phobias.

Before we set off for Cornwall, I did post another letter to Mr Hope-Gapp. There's something easy about sending a letter off before scarpering off on holiday. A lot of redrafting went into each sentence, each phrase, deleting this word, adding that one, remembering to include all the facts, getting the tone right, altering the date so that he won't know how long I spent rearranging it.

So on Sunday, September 30th, we left behind swirls of dog poo in the yard next door for your department to deal with. By the time we return, we hope the mess will have gone. It's a good idea to make yourself scarce when the shit hits the fan—literally in this case. Sometimes I think of the yard as some sort of grotesque art installation. I took another couple of photos on Saturday, before we came away. Maybe if I send them off somewhere they'll win all sorts of prizes because poo is in vogue.

From Poo to Looe—the associations are never far away. Sandy says that Devon is one big canine sphincter, remembering one Bank Holiday in Dartmouth where dog crap was everywhere. But let's cut the crap because I was *so* excited on the train to Liskeard (where we had to change for Looe) and the only sign of my OCD was the overwhelming urge to stroke the velvety crew-cut rising over the seat in front of me (so close do they stack seats on trains these days). I had to forcibly pinch myself, though that crew-cut begged to have a hand through it, but crew-cut-owners aren't renowned for their touchy-feely loved-up personalities, and if I touched it once I'd have had to do it thrice, so I distracted myself with the scenery outside.

Monday—it's wonderful to be away. It reminds me what normal is. My adrenals and everything else take time to be restored but this is instantly therapeutic. This feels like normality and the world back home just a bad dream. We went to Polperro today. We had tea and teacake in a café, we walked round the shops and by the water. It was a good day for Sandy, and he was able to negotiate most places with his bike.

Tuesday—today we looked round West Looe in the morning and in the afternoon we went to the Discovery Centre and sat on picnic tables near the Millpool lake eating chips, which we kept feeding to this duck. It had joined the gulls in the scrum for food. I said to this gull with its head cocked appealingly, 'you can look all you like, you ain't getting any,' because there's these signs up which say *Don't feed the gulls, they can be vicious.* We walked about a bit and returned to our spot and I said, 'that looks like our duck—she's a bit chipped out.' Dot laughed and said, 'You're a scream, Carrie. And how d'you know it's a she?' I said 'Because she-ducks have the mottled markings'. I liked it though when she laughed and said I was a scream. She said I still had that touch of Liverpool in me, the humour, the making people laugh. I like that. Knowing that I've not lost it—because there's not been much to laugh about lately.

Later, we sat on the Banjo Pier and Sandy turned the colour of tea. Not a pale Lady Grey any more, but like a builders' tea shade with evaporated milk added (evappers as my mum used to call it). His legs were tired, as he's been trying to use them, even though he jokes that he needs to get some stabilisers when he walks.

In the evenings we've been doing the Sudokus, racing to see who can complete first. Sandy writes a grid out for us all.

Wednesday—Sandy and I decided to book in at a Bed & Breakfast for the rest of the week so we could spend some quality time together as well as not over-stay our welcome at Ken and Dot's. That's the reason I gave, though if the truth be told I just wanted a bit of downtime with Sandy. I'm not very good in other people's houses, or having them in my own. Plus, its years since we've stayed in a B&B. Our room at the B&B has a wonderful panoramic view, though when you look at it closely, that's its best feature.

Good Points:

1) aforementioned view especially in the evenings watching the lights come up after sunset
2) good drinks selection including Horlicks
3) tray of sweets in the hall (though some of them are a bit soft)
4) DVD player in residents' lounge

Bad Points:

1) crack in the ceiling and above the skirting board
2) TV in the wardrobe
3) no proper carpeting but squares joined together
4) no sink in the en suite bathroom
5) shower old and smelly
6) no little lights above mirrors
7) no tissues
8) no pictures on walls

As you will see, bad points outweigh the good, though I won't let it spoil it for me. We have come away for some peace and quality time.

Thursday—last night I started thinking about the old Posh n Becks for the first time in ages. While Sandy was in the shower I surveyed my bum in the mirror. Different mirrors can make you view your ass anew though it's hard with an ass like Yours Truly. I thought to myself, why can't my bum cheeks be like those perfect unblemished ones in high cut lacy short-pants, like you see in catalogues and magazines? How do they get them to look like that? I suppose being twenty-something, rather than in your mid-life helps, though I don't remember mine ever looking like theirs. But I thought to myself, I know there's a dirty weekend in here somewhere, raring to get out, waiting to kick-start our relationship. Just the fact of being on holiday was doing it for me. I got Sandy going, even though his MS has affected his libido a lot more of late. But then we heard feet thundering above us and the booming voice of a young male laughing at some late night telly programme that put paid to our thrills. I crumpled into repressed hysteria. 'We can't even get away from noise here, for fuck's sake!'

Sandy stroked my hair. 'Don't let it bother you, Carrie.'

But I was already refastening my bra—the noise had totally killed the mood.

At breakfast this morning, we saw the girl-half of the couple. Sandy spoke to her a bit, general chitchat about the weather and what are you doing today. I wished he hadn't. He was condoning their inconsiderate behaviour by not mentioning it.

We mooched about the Looe shops today and I did my best to forget about it all.

Friday—it's like I somehow knew to bring along this journal. I heard the Thunderfeets going out last night and I thought, OK, they're just going for a swift drink at the pub, like they did on Wednesday night. They'll be back by eleven, we'll hear them going to bed, we'll hear their TV, then all will be quiet by midnight. But I couldn't sleep for waiting for them to come in, like I was their parents or something. They finally crashed in at 3 am, talking loud and laughing, no thought or consideration for others, the ceiling above us shaking with each drunken thud. I pounded on the wall in the toilet and shouted for quiet after a while. It was so fucking selfish. We only had four hours sleep, if that. And us coming here to get away from neighbour problems, but instead we've landed a room below the holiday-makers from hell.

Again, only she appeared at breakfast (he was obviously still snoring off his night before). Enter Seroxat Sid. He couldn't contain himself. 'Was that you coming in at three o'clock last night? Because it woke us up.' She said, 'That was Dee, I do apologize.' What could we do? She showed how 'apologetic' she was by stonewalling us for the rest of breakfast (and believe me breakfasts are slow and painful in the circumstances, especially with no other guests around). Sandy tried initiating some conversation but she became monosyllabic, and before long mine and Sandy's conversation with each other dried up, the atmosphere was that prickly.

Saturday—a lovely warm early October day, our last day here. You always want to make the last day special, but we just wanted to absorb the best bits of Looe, East and West, perching on rocks, hanging out at the Banjo Pier, mooching in and out of shops for last minute presents—Christmas already in mind. I wanted to prolong it, eke out every lazy hour, stretch it as far as forever. But I could feel an undertow, a rising panic. The worst thing about holidays is having to go home and as the day advanced and we needed to pack, the dread amplified. A week is lovely but never long enough and you have to leave and go back to your life before. I was getting the Sinking Feeling.

*

On the Sunday, Carrie observes how the Sinking Feeling just got a whole lot worse. She is thinking this during their train journey and then in the taxi home. Dread has taken up residence in her brain and squatted there. Dread of having been away for the week. Dread of what might have happened or not happened in their absence. Dread of coming home to a clump of post hanging through the letterbox, brown envelopes uppermost, and a few on the mat. Dread of letters—especially ones from the Department of Work & Pensions, but even ones from the council with some sort of dismissive response—and the thought of having to process it all, having just returned from a (mostly) welcome break. But before the post, they see the hosed-down yard next door. They see it as a victory as they pass with their luggage, though they can also see—in spite of the half-hearted attempts at cleaning—that the yard still looks untidy. Scuzzy, as Sofe would say. That is the word. Bits of rubbish and loo roll and discarded cartons-cum-dog-toys still fester in the corners. But the council must have said something to the neighbours, that much is confirmed by the reply waiting for them from Liz Fletcher in response to their first letter. It reads:

Dear Carrie & Sandy Cornish

Thank you for your letter of 26th September addressed to my manager, Greg Hope-Gapp. He has asked me to respond, in this instance, to your letter.
I have received another letter as well from a neighbour regarding the barking of dogs. I will be writing to our tenants in respect of these complaints.
Please advise us if the problem continues after the end of this week - after they have received the Council's letter.

Yours sincerely

Liz Fletcher
Housing Resources Officer

Sandy says the tone of the letter is much more receptive than when they wrote in relation to the Tragos, though Carrie isn't so sure. Ms Fletcher mentions the letter from this other neighbour as though without it she might not have taken the complaint seriously. Sandy says it's just their policy and that substantiation is important. Carrie feels he's coming down on the side of the council against her. She also finds Ms Fletcher's words ambiguous. For instance, the sentence *I will be writing to our tenants in respect of these complaints*. Does she mean all of their complaints, including the other noise and the dog-fouling, or does this refer to the dog barking only? Sandy tells her that it's obvious Liz Fletcher means the other complaints as well—why else would the (neighbours) have hosed down the yard? Because of the delays in communication and reaction, Carrie thinks that the other complaint Ms Fletcher is referring to may not be from Priss, but the Onions', remembering the time she coincided with Rick Onions in the alley and he'd talked about the antisocial behaviour and the barking dogs keeping his wife awake.

*

Day Nine

We have been back about a week and although the dog mess was cleaned up for the first couple of days, it is creeping back already. Let me give you a flavour of today, Mr Vowells, which I feel is typical of the annoyance and intrusion we face on a day to day basis. We could hear the dogs crashing about again at 11.45 am.

Sandy thought he heard them in the morning when I was asleep, and yesterday morning too. I'm glad he didn't wake me because once awake, getting back off again is quite an ordeal. My bedside table is full of aids to help me have a comfy night. I have spare earplugs in an attractive little orange-tinted plastic case—almost good enough for jewellery—in case the ones in my ears should pop out in the night and I can't locate them straight away without resorting to dubious gropings under Sandy's thighs while he's sleeping.

I have my water in a sport's bottle because there's nothing worse than waking with a dry mouth in the small hours, though if I sip too much this will result in more trips to the lavatory which triggers off all the loo chain rituals which I believe I've already shared with you. Then there are my nibbles—a bag of nuts—because the mints were heaping further damage on my pearly whites according to my latest dentist. I think he must be a keen golfer when he's not inside people's mouths because he says 'hole in one' and 'hole in two'. Naturally I hate going to the dentist because I feel trapped in the chair. Anyway, the nuts must be good for my teeth because the golfing expressions were absent last time I visited him. I also have a Vick Stick because of my allergies and my bunged-up nose (probably bed mites). Then there's my headache tablets and the White Noise Machine, which is balanced on a tiny stool within reaching distance. And when the Zamoras used to have their all-night parties, I used to have to leave the bathroom light on and door open so that the extractor fan muffled their noise, but the downside was that the light from the bathroom would shine into our bedroom in order to hear the fan so I bought this sleep mask which filters out the light effectively. It looks like a piece of bondage, truth be told, like a black blindfold, though Sandy and I aren't inclined that way. Don't get me wrong, we have practised a bit of S & M in our time—who hasn't?—but it wasn't for us. We felt—well, daft, to be perfectly frank.

Anyway, that is my bedtime routine and I think it is pertinent to this account, Mr Vowells, because it demonstrates all the props needed for a good night's kip.

At 2.10 pm we heard the loud knocking/scraping noises and again at 2.20 pm which sounded like the dogs. Then we heard more noises, which wasn't the dogs this time because the Montego was parked out there.

We tried to sit out in the garden later as it was a nice sunny afternoon. But there were more dog faeces out there, which still haven't been cleaned up, even though the neighbours are home. More flies came over and we had to light chocolate-flavoured incense constantly. We would have sat out longer as the garden is usually lovely at this time of year and this time of day—not too hot—but the smell and the flies put us off.

We could hear clattering and shouting at 4.30. It was the girl shouting (it usually is). Also, a couple of days ago, the cupboards were being slammed really loudly in the kitchen and we heard the girl shouting. I think it was being put on for our benefit because Sandy had been sitting alone in the garden for some time and he told me there'd been no slamming or shouting (she wouldn't have known anyone was there) but the slamming coincided with my appearance and conversation with Sandy in the garden, and so there may be resentment against us because we had to write to your colleagues at the council. In fact, she cut me up in the fast lane of the pavement the other day as she charged along with her chariot-pushchair, just missing my ankles by a hair's breadth. I swear they could feel the wind up on Dartmoor.

Now it's 5.30 pm. Dog faeces still not cleared. More urine out there as well, which stinks to high heaven. The girl has been out there too. I saw her hanging stuff on the line. She had on a pale blue summery top and grey trackies. In our day, bra straps were never seen under a top like that (we wore boob tubes), now they are fashionable, though not grey, twisted ones. My point is, this is another sign of her scuzziness. Sofe says she's a lazy cow, why else doesn't she clean up after her dogs? She has this faint rictus. I thought it was a grin at first, but it's just the way her mouth goes. It's not a smile at all. It's a bit like Sonia out of Eastenders, her mouth does the same when she's annoyed, curling up at the corners. Like a grimace. Is that the word? Just remove the 'ace' and you have what she is. Grim. Or add a 'y' to make grimy.

But anyway, this is all driving me loopy. That may not be a PC word but I wish people would use their imaginations more where mental illness is concerned. It's bad enough for those with physical disabilities, like Sandy, but it's discrimination, surely, to ignore the brain and the heart and the stomach and the bladder and the bowels which, actually, are very physical. Just because the symptoms stem from the brain, why does that have to make them mental anyway? Sandy's stems from the brain too! It will all eventually be found to be due to some dodgy neurotransmitter or suboptimal hormones, just you wait and see.

But the world is more geared towards physical disability. Ask any public venue if they cater for the disabled and they will say yes we have a ramp for wheelchairs or a lift or accessible toilets. But then when you see the symbol for disability facilities it is just that— a wheelchair. Then again, what sign could we put up for the mentally afflicted that would be acceptable? t wouldn't go down well having a figure shouting or hearing voices or trembling—even if it could be represented pictorially—and in what situations would it be used anyway?

That's why I like that meme going round social media that shows an ostensibly abled figure and underneath it reads: *sometimes disability looks like this.*

Day Ten

I woke to the sound of kitchen cupboards being slammed next door. This went on for half an hour this morning. I had a raging headache, a real throbber, and had to take some soluble aspirin. I have started recording the noise on my mobile phone, so that you will hear it for yourself when we send off all this evidence.

The lavatory chain thing is returning, with mutations. Last night I flushed it, the noise of the flushing woke Sandy and he was none too pleased, him having MS and fighting fatigue on a daily basis. But not content with just flushing it once, I had to do it three times. I had to switch the bathroom light on to make sure I'd *really* flushed it. Sometimes I don't believe that it's really flushed because we have a flush that malfunctions and only produces a trickle at times. But actually it wasn't the flushing that woke Sandy, it was the bathroom light. The noise of the light pull is very irritating in the depths of the night. And I had to turn it on and off three times.

But when I returned from the corner shop, sometime after one o'clock, Sandy said he'd heard them next door having a massive row when I was out and could hear them both shouting. Just the mention of it filled me with panic and I felt my legs shake and I couldn't breathe. Sandy needs to proofread an important article he's writing about cuts to welfare, and proofreading is highly stressful and requires his undivided concentration. I was home at two o'clock and still feeling fragile because of my head and a sense of dread that a stressful row might kick off again.

This whole affair is making us both ill and wrecking our whole quality of life. We've gone through this before and it's not fair putting us through it all again, it really isn't. Even after the row had finished and I heard nothing and thought they'd gone out, I couldn't relax. The alarm and distress it causes me (words that are now enshrined in law, Mr Vowells) can stay with me for hours or even days. My body gets psyched up for fight or flight, all adrenals blazing, and the old parasympathetic nervous system takes time to lay down arms. At least, I think this is the scenario, Mr Vowells, though my A level Psychology is steeped in verdigris these days. Noradrenalin comes into it somewhere, I think. That's what the parasympathetic nervous system produces, if I remember rightly, to counteract the adrenalin. But it was like my adrenalin knew to keep on pumping, even though I was standing in the peace of the garden, pruning a withered rose or two, believing them to be out next door, but then I noticed the blind move in the child's bedroom. How did it move by itself? So sleek, so deft. And then I heard the back door open and the girl's voice shouting, 'Look at it! Look at it, you shits!' Not a shout, it was a screech. That's what it was. A mad woman noise. For how were the poor dogs expected to understand? She keeps them captive all day and then screams at them for (presumably) making a dog's dinner of her kitchen. Needless to say they were turfed out into the yard while I fled indoors in a horrible panic, unable to complete the pruning. (Can you report someone for verbal abuse to their pets?)

*

Seroxat Sid goads Carrie to reacquaint herself with the recorder to several ends. Firstly, all that blowing uses up lots of oxygen, in much the same way as deep breathing from the diaphragm which is recommended for anxiety sufferers. Secondly, it concentrates her mind as she squeaks out *Pretty Polly Perkins* or *Wraggle Taggle Gypsies O* in four flats. Thirdly, it stops her from hearing other extraneous noise and, finally, recorders are suitably annoying to others. (There is a top G in *Wraggle Taggle Gypsies)*. She does, of course, check Priss's car has gone before tackling the highest notes. She did play the recorder at school, briefly, but never got beyond the most elementary tunes.

In her next session with Trish, Carrie listens as her counsellor describes her as someone who finds it important to relate to others. Carrie thought all people found this important, but apparently not. Trish gets her to think about what it would be like if she didn't relate to others. ('Try this for a moment, Carrie.') Using her neighbours as an example, Carrie says she finds it surprisingly liberating not having to relate to her neighbours. It makes her feel free and unobligated. Trish nods with something approaching approval.

But not having to relate to neighbours is different than not having to think about them. They constantly intrude through the walls of her home and her mind. She can't help but make comparisons with the Tragos and finds that, for all the Trago noise and clatter which she would never wish to experience again, fundamentally it was that they couldn't cope. Couldn't cope versus couldn't care. These are the two attributes, which distinguishes the one family from the other. This present lot couldn't care, and this is the venal sin. Their presence hangs like a mushroom cloud over her days so that when she is away (like on holiday or visiting her parents) she dreads the sinking feeling that comes with returning. *Watch out for that rising or sinking feeling.* She's got to that stage where she would rather the neighbours were in so she can look forward to their going out; than have them out and dread their return. The silence when they are temporarily absent from home is foreboding and riddled with the weight of an approaching storm—real or imagined.

When she gets home from her session with Trish and hears more reverberations the deep angry voice of conviction that is Seroxat Sid bellows at them to shut up. She never shouts at them face to face—only through walls. Walls give her confidence, even inadequate walls. Yet walls are a prison as well as a protection. It is crazy having noise coming into your house that you can do nothing about. Like suffering domestic violence by proxy. Seroxat Sid's retaliatory shouting is deep and raucous and accompanied by hammering on the walls. Three lots of three. It's the OCD that makes him hammer like that. Or maybe it is Seroxat Sid doing the bellowing and Carrie doing the hammering. Her OCD is overriding the Seroxat. If she ever happens to pass the neighbours on the steps or in the car park area, she'll never refer to the hammering. It's something you can only do through walls but when walls disappear she comes over all embarrassed. Sometimes though, if really pushed, the stroppiness seeps out. She calls it Seroxat Sid. Trish calls it leakage. Feelings that leak out in another manner. Like fidgeting when you're nervous. Maybe her stroppiness will be remembered as stridency when she is dead and buried. A negative made positive. These are sometimes the sorts of qualities people are fondly remembered for, aren't they?

Most evenings, before the news, she plays her

recorder to compete with the intrusions from next door. If she wants to be really annoying Seroxat Sid is called on to play *Tell Mee, Daphne* which reaches a top B flat and doesn't go much lower than a C—that is, an octave above middle C. Sometimes the squeaky notes grate on her, but it's worth it.

Even in her dreams the boundaries are still blurred with the scuzzy neighbours wandering in and out of Number 3 through a connecting door with a flimsy bolt.

The Scuzzies are obsessing her every thought like the Tragos before them, giving her the delusion that she's going insane.

On the Saturday, Carrie is shuffling around the landing in her dressing-gown and there is this tempest brewing in her gut. She already heard the clonk of the letterbox and now she sees a clump of post hanging through its mouth, brown envelopes foremost, like a tongue poking out at her, mocking her. And always on a Saturday.

She feels the soaring dread at the thought of turning over the brown envelopes and seeing The Department of Work & Pensions address on the underside of one of them. She wishes it were Sunday—a safe-from-bills-and-official-letters day. No letters are good letters any more, since the advent of emails. At best they are junk mail or pleas from charities. But she knows—even before pulling out the thick tongue of letters from their maw. Knows that one of them is bad news. That the time has come. The tide is against them—her and Sandy. Her especially, with her invisible illnesses.

The worst is confirmed as the black letters from the Department of Work & Pensions jump out from the back of the uppermost brown envelope in her clutch. It's like they are pursuing her. She is immobile with fear for a few seconds before tearing at the offending letter for daring to arrive. It all has an air of inevitability about it. It is her turn to be 'migrated'—as they call it—from Incapacity Benefit to Employment and Support Allowance. It is a formality. The private health care company will contact her in the next couple of weeks. It all looks very polite and formal and removed. It is devoid of emotion, it is impersonally personal. Sanitised and protected from the shit that results. There's nothing to warn the recipient, nothing to acknowledge how devastating it is with the veiled threat of having your income cut, so veiled, you wouldn't know it was there.

As if she didn't have enough to grind her down without all this. It's not just all the welfare policies that have gone before—it's what's to come. The pulling of the rugs: the cuts to mental health services, the threats to her financial security, the relentless media onslaught describing her and her ilk as fakers, malingerers, scroungers. Not only the media: the chancellor himself said at the recent Tory Conference about commuters getting up at 6 am and looking up at the neighbour's window with the blind still down and sleeping off a life on benefits. He really said those words. She and Sandy and all their disabled friends on social media were incensed. Those remarks were inciting. Sandy said, 'Unfuckingbelievable. Maybe the neighbour works nights and has just gone to bed! Or maybe she's been awake all night in agonising pain! Or maybe he's run out of money on his meter and needs to stay in bed!'

No, it's not the spirit of the Blitz, there's a meanness of spirit, that's turning on the poorer, the weaker, the fragile.

She feels a blog coming on. Her anger filtered through the psyche of Seroxat Sid, aye.

Sid jots down a title: Historic Disability Abuse. He jots down a few opening sentences: *Fast forward twenty years. Bear with me. A judge is looking into allegations of historic disability abuse dating back to 2010. Thousands of people have come forward after a thirty-five-year-old woman forwarded evidence to the police about how her mother was treated on a regular basis by the authorities during that decade. 'In 2013 my mother said that one day we will look back with horror and disbelief about how we treated the disabled. Just as we now look back in sheer disbelief at the way survivors of child abuse and domestic violence, people of colour or people of different sexual orientation were treated not so many decades ago...'*

*

Day Eleven

There was a really explosive row between the Scuzzies, late morning, going on for half an hour. Doors slamming and clattering and dogs barking. It stopped for a while and then there was lots more banging and bashing at lunchtime. The music then went very loud, and I could hear arguing/cupboards slamming when I was in the garden so again I couldn't enjoy the autumn sunshine. I got out my phone and started recording. I don't care what they say in some online forums about recording being seen as a form of harassment. Usually, the types that say such a thing are the ones who have something to hide; the guilty ones. I know that some of you at the council insist on recordings with your own equipment but all of it's evidence, Mr Vowells, and you and those at Shires are always stressing how important it is to collect evidence. This is why I am writing the diary too although sometimes it's hard for words to express the true horror of what we are suffering and the recordings are like a back up—sort of belt and braces, if you like. It is quite impressive when you play it back. It brings home to me just how much that poor house is being abused. Hit and kicked about, when it started off so attractive, even if it's skin was a bit thin. All the more reason to treat it delicately.

I was on the phone a lot between late afternoon and teatime, first to Sofe and then to my parents, and I kept having to get them to repeat what they were saying because of squeals and yells and bumps this end. This may make relentless reading, Mr Vowells, but that's because it *is* relentless. The girl is still shouting 'Cummere Noah! *Now!*' (6.35 pm) and pounding about, plus the dogs are woofing on and off.

They say that incessant barking is a behavioural problem due to dogs being under-stimulated, a bit anxious, and not being *walked*. If they were walked they would use up a lot of their excess energy.

Day Twelve

I know that autumn has everyone's garden in a mess, and we are no exception, but ours is a natural, botanical kind of mess caused by high winds and driving rain, though actually we've had very little in the way of rain so far this autumn—normally we are plagued by thick slugs, black and slimy as a dog's nose. And talking of dogs that brings me to the point of today's entry: next door's have ripped up the black sacks in their garden. There is rubbish and dog do everywhere. It looks atrocious. The dogs are going bonkers for a bit of stimulation. We used to joke, when we lived in Torquay, how even the dogs had ASBOs. Well, these would get a prison sentence! But I am not blaming the dogs in any way. It is not their fault their owners don't know how to look after them. But I took a picture as evidence anyway, Mr Vowells, just so you can see what it's like living next door to a tip.

*

Carrie and Sandy have had what they refer to as the usual blah from someone called Mike Naylor, who is the Housing Resources and Development Manager, following pressure from a councillor they wrote to. The blah consists of sentences like:

> *It is difficult for us to offer any guarantees...*
> *We will investigate what works may be required...*
> *I can assure you we take any antisocial behaviour by our tenants very seriously and would be grateful if you would inform us of any problems that you may experience in the future...*
> *If you wish to discuss this further, please contact me on the above number...*

Carrie decides not to contact him on the above number. Phones are about thinking on your feet, never her strong point, so she will write instead. Sandy says the letter is encouraging. Carrie has reservations, fearing that it is in fact lip service since the councillor put pressure on Mike Naylor to respond. She and Sandy argue about the letter for a while, Sandy suggesting that she will never be satisfied whatever the outcome and that people are being killed in the Middle East.

Carrie sits in a mood, face like thunder. Sandy steers clear of her mood and removes himself from the room. She struts off herself, afraid that she's turning into a fascist nimby when she used to be such a socialist. Live and let live used to be her creed.

She decides to phone Sofe who will understand

because of her own troublesome neighbour—the man who plays his music too loud. It's good to hear Sofe, her animal-loving and fellow anxiety-suffering friend. There is always compassion in Sofe's voice and a touch of vicarious outrage. 'It's ghastly,' she says. 'Ghastly having bad neighbours.'

By the time she comes off the phone, Carrie is fortified. She's in a better mood and will even laugh along if Sandy pokes fun about the way she and Sofe commentate on their illnesses like other people do their social lives. 'I had a bad head day, Wednesday, had a bit of a stomach, Thursday,' he'll often tease, as if these are the main events of their lives. Normally she is quick to retaliate. 'Hullo? Sometimes they *are*?' Today, she half expects him to gibe at her when she returns to the living room but it's as if someone pressed the remote control on him when she was out the room and switched channels.

'We could put a charter through next door,' he says. 'Like we did with the Tragos. We've got no indication that they've ever had one. I'll do it now, if you like.'

This is something they've often discussed, even though it made little difference with the Tragos. But they have thought about a better strategy since then. They have photocopied their own charter in preparation and put asterisks by the relevant bits on the copy, highlighting the behaviours of their neighbours which need amending. Carrie goes to her Shires Housing Association file and retrieves the original charter, as well as the copy with the asterisks. She sees at a glance which paragraphs received the asterisks on the copy.

<u>Noise</u>

* *I agree not to make excessive noise (playing loud music, shouting, slamming doors etc) on or around the* *estate, or do noisy household chores (hoovering, drilling etc) during unsocial hours.*

Dogs

* I agree not to allow any pet for which I am responsible to cause a nuisance through fouling, excessive noise or threatening behaviour.

Carrie expresses her reservations to Sandy about the wording of the first paragraph, which tends to imply that noisy household chores are acceptable during daylight hours. However the first part of the paragraph includes those key words 'shouting' and 'slamming doors'. There are also many other pertinent paragraphs in the charter about children and parking and dog poo bins. All in all, the charter puts the onus back on the resident, its general theme outlining the resident's responsibilities. This concept of rights and responsibilities encapsulates all Carrie used to despise in that it always seemed to be targeting the most vulnerable: claimants, the homeless, the sick. She is appalled to find that here she is now almost embracing the ethos, like a fully-fledged convert.

'OK then?' Sandy heaves himself up onto his stick. 'I'll drop it through their letter- box when I go out to the shops for my bits and bobs. With asterisks or without?'

'Without,' Carrie says. 'Then they won't know it's us necessarily. It could be anybody from the Residents' Association. We'll keep the copy.'

'Without asterisks it is.'

Carrie smiles. When they can take action like this, it makes her feel empowered, like they are doing something, as well as shifting the power back in their direction.

'Give it here.' She takes the original charter from

Sandy. 'Sofe's invited me to pop round…I'll drop it in on the way.'

Although Sofe only lives a few roads away, it is always a big thing for Carrie to leave the house on her own and walk over there. Sofe also knows that Carrie may need to back out, this is understood between them. But as Carrie braves next door's letterbox with the charter, it feels better to be going on somewhere, to shrink the inevitable magnitude this action would bring if she went straight home. She would be sitting there, feeling the uncomfortable silence, waiting, wondering if there would be a reaction; whether the neighbours would guess it was them, whether any shouting or door-slamming would be due to the charter plipping on their doormat. No, it is better she strides over to Sofe's. Take her mind off it all.

On the main road she sees two figures coming towards her. One of them looks like Priss and is that her mother, that sixty-something woman with her beige hair? Carrie turns toward the main road, she will cross it at this point to avoid passing them head on. She's not sure if they've seen her but she scurries over it, just in case.

She is glad to reach Sofe's: to flop into the Indian throws with Sofe's cat and dog sniffing at her ankles.

Sofe is wearing a black dress with a red thread running through the hem, giving her the appearance of a Red Admiral butterfly as she flutters about making them both a green tea—they drink it for its alleged health properties, although neither of them are a fan of the taste. They talk benefits assessments and about how Carrie is waiting for her ESA50 to arrive, any day now. It is all such a worry. She can only face doing a bit at a time.

They discuss their other big worry: neighbours.

'D'you know,' Sofe says, her cat between them now

on the settee, 'the other day I was singing—d'you remember *Life is a Minestrone,* that 10cc song?—well, it was on my mind, and I was singing it as I was making one of my bean-filled cats, I was sewing him up which didn't require much concentration and so I started singing—as you do—Minnie Mouse has got it all sewn up, she gets more fan-mail than the pope, when this raucous out-of-tune voice from next door sang the next two lines—she takes the Mickey out of all my phobias, like signing cheques to ward off double pneumonia—which, as you know, are two of my favourite ever lines. It made me shudder though, Carrie, hearing this jerk commit sacrilege, and it was horribly intrusive, like I couldn't sing privately to myself without someone listening in but I didn't stop singing, Carrie. I didn't let him intimidate me into quiet. I just sang the two lines myself, like I hadn't heard him, and carried on singing in my own time and pace and rhythm.'

Carrie splutters on her tea. 'Good for you, Sofe...ugh, I don't think I could bear that...it's a different sort of intrusion. Sort of creepy.'

Carrie's glad she made it round here. It's good to put her own problems into perspective, to deflate the world over there, back home. Cut it down to size. From here. From this safe distance.

'Hey, Carrie—how about you and Clo come over here for a girlie night on Saturday evening—maybe a meal and a DVD? It's such a long time since we've all had a social evening together.' Carrie is up for that, yes she is. It *has* been such a long time, Sofe is completely right: their anxiety, OCD and phobias preventing a regular social life. But illness can focus too. Restriction may narrow the options but sometimes you can do more with two choices than ten. Ten is overwhelming.

'Don't worry if you're not up to it on Saturday,' Sofe

says as they exchange hugs at the front door, later. This is their code, offering one another a get-out clause, an exit, should they not be well enough. It takes the pressure off and God himself only knows what pressure does to them all.

Carrie delays going home a bit longer. She will get a few things from the shops: a newspaper, some more milk, didn't Sandy say something about needing some more turmeric and spelt bread? She gives him a quick ring on her mobile to check and finds he's not gone out yet. She will save him the bother of going out, she tells him.

She braves the small supermarket, it's a while since she's been here but she wants and needs to prolong going home, to that place of looming thoughts and emotions. She has to hang on to the buoyancy being with Sofe has given her—it will surely crash soon.

In the supermarket, Carrie sees Clo—a rare place for them both to be.

'Wow, I'm seeing you all today!' she tells her other friend. 'Just come straight from Sofe's. She mentioned something about asking us both to hers on Saturday night!'

Clo's face lights up behind her glasses. 'Cool! I could do with a girlie night out—or in.'

Carrie says she could too, to take her mind off the neighbours and (lowering her voice at this point) receiving her letter from the DWP about her migration to Employment & Support Allowance. She knows Clo understands the need to talk in hushed tones, so great is their paranoia of the public perception of claimants. 'I am already filling out an old dummy form in pencil, trying to prepare my answers before the real form comes.' Clo puffs in response, enraged as they all are about the whole rigmarole and the extra anxiety it puts on them. Carrie says, her voice rising, 'Why can't they leave vulnerable people like us alone?'

Vulnerable people, my arse.

But where did that voice come from? Carrie was so careful to scan the aisles but shoppers come and go and in the space of a blink the scenery can change.

Clo is looking over Carrie's shoulder in the direction of the voices, coming from the oils and condiments direction.

So she can go out then.

Carrie turns to see a familiar face, unsmiling now, and another older face, almost foaming at her.

Priss and an older lady.

Carrie feels Seroxat Sid rising inside her, trying to get out. Sid is here, never fear. He has been rattled. 'What is your problem?'

Priss waves her hand, as if she has no more appetite for this, but the older lady with her—Priss's mother—is just warming up.

'People like you,' says the mother with hair that Carrie now sees is a kind of grond: a cross between grey and blond. 'You're the problem.'

'Leave it mum.' Priss attempts to lug her mother away but Mrs Priss is having none of it. She is pointing a grim finger.

'It's people like you…getting freebies from the government and taking it away from genuine people. Like my granddaughter outside in her wheelchair.' Her voice is becoming shrill. 'She can't even come in here because the pigging aisles are too narrow.'

Seroxat Sid is boiling over. 'Genuine people?'

'Yes. The truth hurts, doesn't it? I've seen you—you're just taking the piss, people like you, and making genuine people like my granddaughter suffer—'

Seroxat Sid is apoplectic. He will surely have a brain haemorrhage any moment with all that blood rushing to his brain. 'How does it feel to be one of the baying mob, then, missus? Swallowing all that bum fodder in the Daily Hate Mail and the Daily Ex-Lax?'

The eyes of Mrs Priss are like sour grapes. 'You're nothing but a scrounger—my daughter's seen you. I've heard you, do you think I haven't?'

'Heard me?'

'Mum! Leave it. Please.'

Clo's glasses have steamed up and her cheeks are glowing with ire. 'Carrie, don't rise to it…they've been brainwashed.'

And Seroxat Sid is wanting to lamp the older woman on her grond bonce. It's all he can do to control his pumped fists and he has to make do with the words he shouts behind him as Clo tries to lead him away from the situation: 'Why don't you just get back to your scratching post, eh? You vile woman.'

When she returns home, Carrie is shaking with anger and fresh tears. She furnishes Sandy with the details when she's calmed down sufficiently, though she feels her blood still smouldering. He does his best to defuse it. 'We're all up against it with the press as it is. But you stood up to them, by the sounds of it. Be pleased with yourself, Carrie. I'm sure you did yourself proud.'

Yes, he is right. She did it alone, more or less, though the presence of Clo undoubtedly helped. But it took guts. And she would like to enjoy being pleased with herself, for standing up against injustice and propaganda, making that feeling last.

But the following day comes the white envelope containing her ESA50, with its rectangular tongue raping through the letterbox. Unwanted. Unwelcome. Forced.

But Carrie has been expecting it. She has her answers prepared so that she can meet the four week dreadline. Dreadline? Yes, everyone knows that's what it is.

She begins copying out from her rough copy what she has written for the section headed 'About Your Illnesses or Disabilities'.

Because of my agoraphobia, anxiety and social phobia, I need to be at home most of the time. I need to be able to escape a distressing situation as I feel trapped in public places if I can't escape. I'm unable to go out every day. When I do go out my partner accompanies me most of the time and understands my needs. If I am out and get distressed then he calms me down eg if I get agitated and start shouting. I do shout when I am agitated. I get dizzy and breathless when I'm distressed and can't see or walk straight or think straight. I fear collapsing. I need to be near a wall, or sit down or get to a place of safety. I can't drive because of panic attacks and fear of blacking out. I am on 20 ml Seroxat daily for my anxiety and phobias. I also take Diazepam (5 mg). I occasionally take a homeopathic remedy called Kali Phos. although I have lost faith in it. Over a period of time stress and anxiety builds up. If I am too over-loaded or stressed I shut down or go into meltdown and can't cope. I need recovery time and to pace myself to keep this at bay otherwise I go downhill.

My OCD is getting worse. I get stuck having to do things three times. Or I must do something before the kettle boils. Or if I phone my friend and there's no answer, I have to let it ring 12 or 14 times but not 13. A double ring counts as one. I am terrified of germs and door handles and phones that other people might have touched... there are so many superbugs around now...

Is this good enough? Is this bad enough? For that's what they'll be judging her on. How bad she is. Is she bad enough not to work? What is work anyway? She sees people working their socks off for free: volunteering at shops, helping their loved ones, painting their pictures, recording their guitar-accompanied songs and giving legal or indeed welfare advice advice online. Giving it all away, for love, for free, for nothing…it is not something-for-nothing, as these politicians and media moguls keep spouting until their poison has burrowed into the sleepy brains of Priss and her grond mother and thousands upon thousands every day. Wake up! The big society is alive and kicking and it's on Facebook and YouTube and Twitter. It is a nothing-for-something society. It is one full of unsung heroes. She and Sandy are a part of it: they are admins in a Facebook Group, giving others benefits advice, when they can. She thinks of Sofe's crafted cats she spends hours making and usually gives away to friends and family.

She lays down her form, exhausted.

To be continued, she thinks.

Another time...

*

Day Thirteen

In this situation it is OK to have a Day 13, because that is the number that comes after 12 and I don't have a choice. It doesn't come from the same place as the choice I have when deciding how many rings to listen to before putting down the phone.

But I had a dream the night before last, Mr Vowells,

of the older dog, Paddy. He was looking up at me (which he sometimes does from next door's yard with sad eyes) and he spoke to me. He said 'Help me'. I told Sandy about this dream, and you'll see the significance in due course. You see, this must be one of the worst days since our neighbours in Number 4 moved in because now our nights are being disturbed, and not just by the dogs chasing things over the slate floor. Sandy and I were both abruptly torn from our sleep at 3.15 am by yelling, loud noises and sudden bangs and slamming doors. There was one almighty smashing noise—poor house, sounded like it was having its bones broken. I wished I could soothe it and give it some love and therapy. Then the child started running about and squealing. This went on for about two or three hours. We had on the white noise machine but the noises penetrated. We rapped on the wall for quiet but we were ignored. In retrospect, if we'd have known it was going to go on half the night we would have called the police as I'm sure they'd classify it as a domestic, only you don't always think clearly when it's the middle of the night. Because I kept thinking it would die down—I didn't think anyone was in immediate danger and I didn't want my sleep disturbed on any account because it's so long since I've had a social night with the girls, and one thing which would spoil it for me is lack of sleep and having to deal with the police. I don't function without sleep. I get dizzy and disorientated, and the most terrible headaches. I may sound like just another Seroxat Sid but this is the reality for me. I had to take a tranquilliser on top but that didn't help me sleep either and I started pulling my hair out. Literally, hair by hair.

Anyway, at something to five this morning I heard this awful cry from a dog outside. I said to Sand, 'It sounds as if a dog's been run over'. Then some time after—I don't know how long—I heard someone whistling for a dog and calling its name. I'd given up on sleep by this time, so I went to the window and lifted the curtain and I saw the girl from next door in her pyjamas calling 'Pepper' several times. She went running onto the pavement and eventually she came back with Pepper. She was bending down to his level to guide him back because she didn't have a lead. She just had her hand cuffed around his neck. We could still hear doors banging on and off and we didn't get back to sleep until around 7 am. I realized I'd fallen asleep because I had a dream of the girl and she was pushing a supermarket trolley, she pushed it into the road, quite deliberately, and a toddler was knocked down and killed. The scene then changed to a hospital, and there was the girl, it was a mental hospital, I believe, and I realized the girl was quite mad. I was told that she was making complaints against us, and I remember feeling gobsmacked but it all made sense, because she was not the full shilling. She may have had a bandage, or sling, or cuts to her face, I can't quite remember now.

But I felt dreadful in the morning. I didn't get up till gone eleven. I had this awful spinning sensation when lying down, like you do when you're drunk, only I wasn't drunk. I couldn't sit up without the merry-go-round. Nothing merry about it though. Bang goes my meal with the girls at Sofe's. The last time we all went out together was at one of the socials, organized by a fellow sufferer from one of Trish's groups. Someone called Angela. She was our age, but oh so conventional. We turned up at this dippy, patronizing party and Angela had organized this Crazy Auction where people bought raffle tickets and won silly prizes like tins of beans, and cheesy perfumes, and there was Pass the Parcel with naff prizes, but it was the notion of fully grown women (and they were all women at the party) playing this kindergarten game and getting just as excited as any five-year-old, and Sofe and I looked at each other with the Face. The Face is a code instantly understood by both of us and consists of brightened, incredulous eyes, as if to say, Oh. My. God. So, I think I'm due a decent night out, Mr Vowells, as nights out are few and far between. And good nights, they're an endangered species.

But I staggered up and out to the shops because I had to go out and once I was out I didn't want to come home again because I don't feel my home is my sanctuary any more, but I've said it before and I'll say it again. Home is important for people like us because we need to spend a lot of time in it. Furthermore, we only posted a charter through the neighbours' letterbox the other day so ignorance is no defence. And I keep worrying about Paddy. He asked for my help in my dream and I feel I let him down. I fear he may be dead and I should have contacted the RSPCA back in the summer as my friends advised. I should have listened to my dream the night before last. It was a warning. A cry for help. A premonition. My mum's always said I have a bit of the psychic in me. In any case, Sandy and I now need to draft a letter to Mike Naylor as somewhere in all his blah he did assure us he takes antisocial behaviour seriously and said he'd be grateful if we would let him know if there were any further incidents.

Oh and I've now also received my ESA50 form to fill out and if I lose my benefits because of not being able to complete it properly, I won't be accountable for my actions.

*

Carrie and Sandy see neither hide nor hare of the Scuzzbags (the name for their neighbours that has now stuck) for a few days, though they still post the letter off to Mike Naylor anyway. But the quiet is a teasing reminder of what life could be like, and yet Carrie feels her shoulder and neck muscles tensing in anticipation of their return, which is four days later. She thought—hoped—they might have split up, after their mother of all rows.

The following morning, Carrie only sees one of the dogs go out in the yard for his business. It's Pepper, confirming her suspicions that Paddy is dead. It gives her that Sinking Feeling. That cry the other night, that was the dog being run over, he escaped in the blaze of the Scuzzbags' row, and that'll be why the Scuzzbags have been absent for a few days. They'll have been with their respective families.

But if she thought, with blood on their hands, they might have learned their lesson from their selfish deeds, if she thought they might be contrite, she was on course for a rude awakening. Within a few days the same noises start to occur once more: doors slamming, child screaming, footsteps thumping, and the remaining dog crashing about, confirming for her what she's always suspected—that Pepper, the younger spaniel, is the one making all the noise; is the liver-and-white eruption. She's seen him in the yard, circling round and round, never keeping still, like he's got ADHD arising from his lack of exercise. If his behaviour outside is anything to go by, it is he who is the manic one, hurling himself into chairs and furniture in the kitchen, clattering dog bowls across the slate floor, whereas Paddy is (was?) content to sit still, to play only if pushed. But what is Pepper without his companion?

Carrie now has new examples to put on her ESA form, though her writing is scrawl. She steps up her recorder playing. She is the whistle-blower. She sort of understands where the mad little dog is coming from and squeaks out *Tell Mee, Daphne* again and again, sometimes leaving a gap, so that the Scuzzbags will think it's stopped, then she'll repeat it. Sometimes she just goes up and up the scale, to see how far she can go. She knows recorders can drive people potty, especially if not played properly. She can feel Sandy being driven mad, shouting at her to stop.

'Put it to me in writing,' she shrieks. This is what it's doing to them. He starts to put on their hi-fi, quite loud. 'You can't do that!' She tries to suppress her raised voice. 'You can't.' If they play their music loud, they'll be giving the green light for their neighbours to do the same, then it'll escalate. Then it'll be tit-for-tat. But they can't give up now, not when they've been the face of reason for so long. That's the face they've shown to the authorities and they must keep it up.

'Put it to me in writing, put it to me in writing.' Sandy's childish parody of what was meant to be an attempt at black wit, only adds fuel to the fire as she pulls the plug on the music. 'To hell with living like this,' Sandy shouts. 'I want some mari-joo-wana.'

He levers himself up and hirples out. She knows that he's going to score some marijuana off Mrs Hug-a-Tree, Eden's mother from Number 8. The 'herbal medicine' helps his MS. Carrie used to like Fiona Hug-a-Tree until she went to her yoga class where Fiona would hug everyone around Carrie while forgetting Carrie herself. It wasn't even intentional, Carrie reflects, just a symptom of Fiona Hug-a-Tree's woolly-headedness. Like the time Carrie explained to her that the reason she sometimes had to miss yoga was due to her poor health, to which Fiona Hug-a-Tree said, don't worry, I'm used to you floating in and out, making Carrie sound like she was what her mother would call a flibbertigibbet. Though she loved yoga, Carrie felt misunderstood and unhuggable and duly left the class. The fact that Fiona hasn't enquired after Carrie or even noted her absence is confirmation to Carrie that she is dispensable.

Carrie plucks out a strand of her hair.

Another.

And another.

She likes to lick each hair as she pulls it out and add it to the pile. It's a guilty secret. The pile grows daily, soon there'll be enough to make a wig. She likes to see it all there. She likes the sharp pull of it as it comes out. It grounds her like the news grounds her. Items plucked from the body of world news, which sometimes hurt, but only momentarily, and sometimes give pleasure, but only momentarily.

She paces. The house is surely a prison. If she could just take a few paces away from the house and make it shrink in significance. She has no reason to venture out into the environs except to wrap up the compost waste—a few days' worth—and transfer it to the compost bin. She doesn't have to check the plugs or the iron or the locks, she tells herself, this is only round the block, round the block, round the block. She mutters the refrain on her way to the compost bin but when she raises its brown lid she finds rubbish in there: ordinary refuse—old cans, and dog food tins as well as ripped cardboard boxes of smelly meat—and the bottom of the bin is swimming with hundreds of maggots. The urge to barf is slightly less than the desire for revenge. *Right! You wait!* She takes hold of the boxes of rubbish, that which she can bear to touch, and kicks them over in the direction of the Scuzzbags' bins—so they'll know that she knows. Is it malicious? Or just another example of their clueless, thoughtless behaviour? But there's still the question of what to do with the maggot-infested bin. She and Sandy have looked after their bins; have been meticulous about their recycling. They have collected newspapers so they can parcel up their waste securely. At once she starts to wheel the maggoty bin over to the Scuzzbags' compost bin. She will do a straight swap. But when she lifts the lid, it smells dubiously of dog poop, even though the dog poo bins are the proper depository for canine waste. She wants to weep. The maggots make her squeamish and retchy, she doesn't want them in her bin, they don't belong to her. She looks to the other bins at the top of the flight of steps between Number 4 and 5 and swiftly exchanges bins with the Onions'. Good move. The Onions' will work out who they think the filthy rubbish belongs to and will be fellow adversaries of the neighbours-from-hell.

She returns indoors, scrubs her hands eighteen times (eighteen is a good number) and phones Sofe to tell her about it, apologizing again for having to miss the meal the previous Saturday when she was so looking forward. Sofe is totally understanding about it, especially after hearing more about the awful night Carrie was subjected to. Sofe says she would have been just the same and reminds Carrie that she has had to cancel social engagements due to illness. They have this understanding that nobody is letting anyone down.

As for the compost bins, Sofe says that it is illegal to dump waste in another's bin—the recycling helpline told her so. This only adds more ire to Carrie's campaign and she goes back outside—*you need to get out more*—first of all standing outside her front door, then walking past her own kitchen window until she is on the perimeter of the Scuzzbags' property. She is outside their sitting room windows. All she has to do is stretch out a fist and knock on the glass until one of them raises a net curtain. It is easier knocking on a window than a front door. Less formal. She climbs into the skin of Seroxat Sid. Has a fleeting fantasy of him crashing an axe through the pane. She can understand why people are driven to this. Seroxat Sid would just get on with it. She hears his deep whisper, 'I've got an axe,' hears it thrice, his whisper becoming louder as he puts his face up to the window, brings his hands together and swings the chopper, just as Mrs Onions passes, turning round as if to say, What the hell are you doing? Carrie imagines tomorrow's headlines: Seroxat Sid slays selfish slobs.

Still in the skin of her alter-ego, Carrie looks on as Seroxat Sid marches back the way he came with his bloodied axe, passes his own house, and Priss's, and Number 1, he's running rings round them all, passing all the back gates, even his own, until he comes to the bin area for Number 4. He has this compulsion to march round the block another three times (incurring further peculiar glances from the Onions woman who is now by her car, as well as peculiar looks from two of the three pillars forming the front portico of Number 2 and 3—the end one, and the middle one which they share with Priss, having been cleaned and shined up as white pillars should, leaving the third pillar, Seroxat Sid's, looking pitiful and squalid with its years of verdigris). On his third time round, passing the battered trellis, Seroxat Sid retreats into the back-seat of Carrie's imagination because Paddy is there. Paddy! Still alive! Though the poor dog can hardly stand up on his back legs, which are shaved of fur, indicating an operation.

*

Day Fourteen

Mr Vowell's...this is what I'm having to do, complete my

ESA50, which, as you may be aware, is the form for people who are unable to work...and I am struggling with it...I am struggling to know what the difference is between coping with expected change and unexpected change...all change is unexpected, surely...I cannot for the life of me think of an example of expected change, though they give an example of a change of an appointment time but if you are expecting to see your doctor at one time and then they change it, that is unexpected, and sends me into a spin...it is all designed to trick us out of our entitlements, of course...and we are entitled...no matter how much the media are slating what they call 'the entitlement culture' in an effort to be a mouthpiece for the government and their austerity agenda.

But I wonder, Mr Vowells, do *you* have to hear what I do?...the shouting and rowing at lunchtime...needing a white noise machine on constantly?...maybe your salary affords you better walls, with more robust insulation...but I can hear my neighbour again...any noise is change from a quiet baseline...I suppose we now expect the noise so maybe that's what they mean by expected change...but I can hear my neighbour shouting...Noah, geddere! Noah, geddout!...always shrieking at the poor kid...now there is intermittent bleeping of a smoke alarm...banging doors...knocking noises and more doors slamming...haven't been able to get on with anything properly, Mr Vowells...feel wound up, on edge and stressed by it...what it the point of doing anything else but this...the world population is too large, this is the conclusion I've come to...I've done my bit by not having children...but am I rewarded for it, in incentives and bonuses?...I couldn't have a baby anyway, my threshold for pain is too low, and Sandy's tadpoles are probably stuffed by now and that's just the physical side...my mental side couldn't cope with it either, not with my anxiety and my OCD...what good would I be to a child?...I am just Seroxat Sid...but so many people override the facts of their minds and their bodies and then you end up with neighbours-from-hell who shouldn't have had kids in the first place...but over-population and the battle for space is leading to neighbourhood problems, Mr Vowells, because we all have to be stacked like sardines in houses with jerry-built walls.

But I wonder, Mr Vowells, why you haven't asked to see this log yet?...did you just forget?...is it that you're too busy?...but it's been ages now since you asked us to write it for a month...maybe I'll just send it to you, because your impression must be that everything is hunky dory here because I'm not sure how much one department down at the council communicates with the other.

Day Fifteen

The child has taken to running around and squealing a lot. The thumping footsteps are just like when the Tragos were here, except there's only one of him. The smallest children can make the biggest noise. In fact, I'd say the smaller the child the bigger the noise. He should be running outside but of course he can't, can he? Not with all that dog do. The footsteps from hell went on constantly from 10.30 this morning. Why don't these people take their children *out*? I would break in and bubblewrap his feet if I could.

In fact I was on the phone trying to ask advice about ear defenders of all things, you know, like workmen wear. But I couldn't *hear* myself think for all the noise next door. How ironical is that? I swear she is jumping up and down on the floor with him, just to annoy. So I had to come off the phone, my query unresolved, and I flung our back door open and stomped outside and up our back steps so I could see over the fence. Her back door was wide open even though it's November, and noise spills out when doors are open, but I didn't wait, I launched straight into my tirade about how I couldn't hear myself on the phone and couldn't she control her brat? The brazen face stared back at me before morphing into something more retaliatory. 'Buy him a rubber mat then,' she snarled, as if somehow neighbour consideration and soft furnishings are someone else's responsibility. Then she darted inside her house, with a bone-shaking slam of her back door. Sandy was at the MS Centre in Exeter so enter Seroxat Sid's fist which collided with the wall—his right fist with the letters h-a-t-e tattooed on each knuckle. Then he departed and I fell into a heap of angry and frustrated sobbing, loud enough for the Scuzzy bitch to know the effect she was having on my mental health.

But maybe that only gives her the upper hand, knowing she has broken me, as they all have. She cranked up her music, the bass pounding in time to my headache and the blood being pumped furiously around it. I didn't know what to do, I must have looked like Munch's Scream, my hands over my ears, my mouth stretched in horror. I knew I shouldn't have done it. I was now just as guilty of heaping hurt on these walls. I pity these walls, what I have done to them this side, treating them like a punchbag. I hate what our neighbours have done to theirs on the other side. These walls are surely bruised and scarred. They are surely unhappy and hurting. They have surely absorbed all the badness, like a child with a woeful upbringing. They surely need some healing hands to rid them of the pain and negative energy festering between the struts, otherwise it will stay there for the next people. Mr Vowell's, I wanted to say sorry to the walls, there and then. I wanted to repair any ill feeling toward them but I was utterly defeated. Whatever I did for them this side wouldn't be mirrored on the other, so what was the point? Angry bass beats were still pounding against them from *there*. I think I downed a few tranquillisers at that point and something for my headache and as soon as they started to take effect Seroxat Sid was back with a vengeance. Ha! He was calmer now, he opened up his kitchen drawer, the one where he keeps bits of string and AA batteries and screwdrivers and other odds and sods, and he found the little pale blue plastic key, the generic one that opens all electric meter cupboards everywhere. He then stomped round the corner of the building, key in fist, to the place where the meters to Number 4 are housed. He couldn't be seen as the only overlooking windows are the upstairs side windows of the Scuzzies and the Onions'. But even if the Scuzzy bitch happened to be standing there, she'd have had to have her nose pressed right against the window as the meters are directly beneath. She wouldn't have heard Sid coming anyway because of the crashingly loud din from her hi-fi.

Oh but that was a sweet satisfying moment for Sid as he bent down, fixed the triangular shaped female bit over the same shaped male bit in the meter's door, turned the lock and pulled the door open. There was the big red switch, giving it large, feeding all the electricity to the house. Just one upward push and—silence!

Stealthily he crept away before the fallout. He kept on walking, quickly, along the main road, across it and into Dart Close. By the time I got to Sofe's house, Sid had fled and I was shaking with panic, sheer triumph and utter exhaustion. I flopped down there and slept off my headache.

Day Sixteen

We were woken in the small hours again (2 am) by shrieking, bumps and a door being slammed repeatedly which made the whole house shake to its foundations. We had the white noise machine on, too. Heard her shouting, 'Get out, or I'll call the police' (or words to that effect) and we heard him say, 'You're mad' though we could hear her voice much louder than his. I agree with him. She *is* mad. She must be. I know it's not PC to say such a thing, especially me with all my problems but someone who is a bit mad shouldn't be just dumped there and left to get on with it, without support. We also agreed with her in that we would have called the police too if they hadn't have shut up. But then we saw him leave. We heard her continuing to shout (further evidence of her madness, Mr Vowells, for if he wasn't there, who was she shouting at? Her child? But why shout at him if she disturbed his sleep?) The noise was fit to wake the dead, Mr Vowells, but no one hears it but us. We are the only semi-attached victims. The Onions' have the alleyway running between their house and Number 4. They are protected by fresh air. Except it's not so fresh now, it pongs to high heaven. The long and short of it is, I didn't get to sleep till something to five for fear of it kicking off again. I was wound up and stressed and I took two tranx. This isn't a well state, it's a hell state. I feel like killing them. I can understand why people want to put an axe through their neighbours' wall, through their heads. Today I feel absolutely shattered. Went to bed at 4.30 pm, though haven't been able to sleep because of the loud dragging furniture noises. It's tantamount to psychological assault, Mr Vowells. They are surely taking the wee wee. I should know. I can always produce wee wee, any hour, any minute, call it a freak of nature, and I have to count fast up to at least seventy or eighty while weeing because the number I reach is the number of years I will live. I will force another trickle out and race through the count if perchance I should run out of wee before I've got to the magic seventy or eighty, otherwise I get this overwhelming sense of doom (or else I'll change the rules, then everything is semi OK again). But you know my most intimate habits by now, Mr Vowells, and that is humiliation enough for anyone.

Day Seventeen

Last week a film crew came, Mr Vowells. This was the one that our neighbour Priss must have contacted a few weeks ago regarding participating in a programme about the neighbours, that is, our neighbours and their dog mess in Number 4. I say crew but it was really only one man, plus his camera and recording equipment. But he introduced himself, and said he was making a programme about neighbourhood issues and breakdowns.

'One of your neighbours wanted to participate so we're inviting other neighbours around and about for their input and their side of things,' he said.

'Oh yes. We know about it, ' I volunteered. 'Our neighbour, on that side, said she was going to contact you about the dog mess and all the rest of it over there.' I hitched my thumb in the general direction of Number 4.

The man chatted to us for a while and invited us to give our written consent and blah-de-blah. But when the camera started rolling and the microphone was switched on I fell mute and left it largely to Sandy. I don't want to be on TV but our chap reassured us that only a fraction of it would be used. He asked us lots of questions and took pictures of next door's garden, and said he'd invited them to be interviewed too, as well as other nearby neighbours, to give all sides. He said everybody has a side and a take on a situation that may be different from ours. He asked us if we'd have a problem with that and we said not at all, because as you know we are reasonable people, and it's usually unreasonable people with things to hide that object or decline. However, our neighbours weren't available for interview, he said, which didn't surprise Sandy or me one jot. They know they don't have a side viewers will sympathize with.

Anyway, he left us his card and contact number, should we need to contact him further.

Day Eighteen

It's in the paper, Mr Vowells.

Sofe told me and I got a copy for myself today.

I have photocopied it for you.

You will see the headlines: *Dog badly injured in hit-and-run.*

And although it states that the police are 'hunting for a callous hit and run driver whose white Transit van mounted a pavement and badly injured a dog', Sandy and I both know this is a lie. If you read the article carefully you will see that it doesn't add up. Yes, Paddy, their Springer Spaniel was *thrown across the road and left in agony with a broken pelvis in the early morning incident on October 27th*, that much is true, as we've already documented. But there was no van, and as for the bit that says Samantha Steer *mature student* (I will return to that in a bit) *faces a £2000 vet's while Paddy has a six-week battle to full recovery* and that *her son Noah owns the dog*, well, me and Sandy almost choked. Most of it is distortion or outright fabrication. Like the bit about her partner Spencer Woodcock walking the dogs early in the small hours of the morning because *someone has been around the place winding the dogs up and the only way to keep them quiet is to take them for a walk.* I mean, does that ring true?

Sandy said, 'Well if the Transit did mount the pavement it'll have been to avoid a loose dog—or dogs—belting hell-for-leather in the middle of the road.'

And *Mature student*? She's neither mature, nor student, Mr Vowells. I've seen neither file nor folder within shouting distance of that house. It's all lies. Or misleading. Like the way she makes out her son *owns the dog*. Hullo? He's all of two. Is that playing the public sympathy card or what? The public will have the boy down as eleven or twelve. *They face a £2000 vet's bill.* It's an appeal for money towards the bill, which they can't afford to shell out for, but they can't admit it's their fault because they are legally to blame if accidents occur as a consequence of their irresponsibility (dogs not on a lead) so they've come up with this scam. They've manipulated the press, because people reading this will see them as nice, caring dog-lovers who are victims of this heartless driver. But we know the truth. That's me, Sandy, and now you and your council colleagues, Mr Vowells, because you have it on record that we wrote about that wall-shaking row that night. And if I was that newspaper reporter I'd have smelt a rat. I'd have known it didn't add up. I'd have wondered why someone was walking a dog in the small hours of the morning for starters. Because the fact is they *weren't* walking their dogs at all, and their justification for walking them just doesn't ring true. This is the real giveaway statement from her: *People say 'didn't you get the number plate?' but that wasn't what you were concentrating on. It wasn't until the lead had gone from your hands that you realised*

167

what happened. It's because there was no lead. We saw her running after Pepper, the other dog, bending down to his level, and guiding him back by his neck. Sandy said that the fact that she suddenly talks in the second person shows that she was concealing a lie. I mean, why didn't she say, 'It wasn't until the lead had gone from my hand that I realized what had happened' or 'from Spencer's hand'? Though even that would be an odd way of putting it. I mean, can you imagine it, this Transit van, mounting the pavement in the small hours when the roads are empty and knocking the lead out of someone's hand? Do me a favour. Well, we did contact the police. Just to get it logged. We did it anonymously. But they didn't seem that interested.

*

Carrie is unable to process all the wars and battles featured daily on the news, any more. There is only one battle on her mind now. All has gone deathly quiet again next door, but her nervous system is always gearing up for action. Maybe the Scuzzbags have really split up this time. She wishes it were true. She can't figure it out. She keeps checking at the window, unable to enjoy the quiet, and now she's seen a car in her and Sandy's parking space. If only she'd not looked out, then she could have remained in ignorance. This unauthorized parking makes her see red (though if the opportunist had taken the Scuzzbags' space, she'd have overlooked it. Nay, she would have positively encouraged it). Seroxat Sid whooshes under her skin, marches out and circles the car, round and around, surveying its insides, before returning indoors on a mission. People are always taking liberties. If it was the Morris Minor that occasionally parks in their space—a friend of Melvyn Styles in

Number 1—Sid wouldn't be so angry, Morris Minors being nice cars, ergo their owners. But this isn't the Morris Minor, ergo a lesson needs to be taught. Well put, Seroxat Sid. With the Latin and all.

When Carrie emerges again from her back gate, she catches sight of Louann Onions chatting to a man who looks a bit familiar. There's something conspiratorial about their body language. Carrie thinks they may see something odd about her, something repelling. On the rare occasions she ventures into town, sometimes she has this sense of people avoiding her, slightly scared by her. She doesn't know if she likes this feeling any more. She's more scared than any of them. Louann Onions and the man disappear through the Onions' back gate. As they do so Seroxat Sid returns, striding over to the trespassing vehicle. He takes out the scrap of paper from his pocket and writes on it in big angry letters —THIS IS A PRIVATE PARKING SPACE. PLEASE SHIFT YOUR CAR NOW OR I'LL CALL THE POLICE—before wedging it under the nearside windscreen wiper of the offending vehicle.

It's a bad egg this month, Carrie is certain. She understands she gets these every so often. What's the use of eggs any more? She realizes hers will never be fertilized and it doesn't trouble her. The only thing that troubles her about them are a) the fact that she still has to put up with the pain regardless, since there's nothing in nature which allows you to opt out, no switch to stop the eggs from their relentless monthly journey, and b) the consequences of other people who went through with egg fertilization and have spawned noisy brats. Sandy doesn't regret not having children, at least that's what he's often told her, though sometimes she wonders if he does.

They met initially through a personal ad—she placed

it in a Pagan publication and he replied. He said he wouldn't mind having a child when they first met, though later he said he was just saying that because he thought she wanted one. She'd been a bit obsessed about having a child when in her thirties, but as soon as someone was prepared to take her up on it, she bottled it. The Pagan way was to celebrate the woman's fertile body, pregnancy, birth, new life. It all seemed beautiful and natural and romantic. But Carrie couldn't live up to it, and gave up on the idea. She had deluded herself that she could cope with the all the pain and the stress. So she and Sandy marked the festivals and changing seasons instead—the baby became symbolic. The birth of the new moon, the new year, the growing light, the new shoots.

Now, the rituals have all but dropped away. They are out of touch with all that. They barely even light a candle these days. One of the biggest fire festivals—Samhain—passed them by and they hardly gave it a second thought. She and Sandy are growing apart. In fact, she writes more intimately to Mr Vowells. The thought of Mr Vowells makes her more determined. 'I'm going to send my journal off to Mr Vowells soon,' she says, more to herself than anyone. 'See if I don't.'

If Sandy's heard her, he doesn't seem that interested. He's more absorbed with something going on outside, like he's waiting for something or someone to appear. When, twenty minutes later, he hears the sound of voices he lifts himself up with his stick and staggers to the window. 'There's that guy from the film company. He must have been back to interview some other people.'

Carrie joins him at the window. It's the man Carrie saw earlier, talking to Louann Onions. She knew she recognized him. She wants to run out after him and tell him about the latest neighbour escapades—the massive rows, the badly injured dog, the lies to the newspaper—

though if he came into their house now, he would hear jack shit from the Scuzzbags' direction. If he looked over into their garden, all would be clean. She thinks about intercepting him anyway regarding the exact transmission date for the programme, but Louann Onions is out there in the parking area giving him the final scraps of her version, her eyes casting subtle backward glances to her various neighbours' houses in turn—at least, that's how it seems from where Carrie's standing. The middle-classness of the Onions' scares Carrie. Middle class people aren't cowed by her strops. They fight back with self-assuredness. Then, just as the man prepares to get into his car—the one Sid was circling earlier—both he and Louann Onions catch sight of the irate note jammed under the windscreen wipers.

*

Carrie stands with her ear to the wall. She hears little knocks, this morning, like heels clipping the laminate floor next door. They are back. The footsteps trampling over her quiet and short-lived enjoyment of her home. If it was in your own house, you would tell it to stop.

Standing in this strange posture, not just with her ear but her whole trunk flattened against the wall, she realizes she must look a bit batty, and isn't that Louann Onions passing? Is it possible that she can see in? Carrie quickly adjusts a painting on the wall, reminding herself of John Cleese in the psychiatrist episode when he's trying to confirm his suspicions about the people in the bedroom next door until he's caught earwigging. 'Just checking the walls.' She can now see Louann Onions and Priss chatting and laughing along together. How can this be? How can they be so relaxed together—two neighbours, both newer to the neighbourhood than she and Sandy? It's them—she and Sandy—they're the ones, surely. The ones who should be at the epicentre, with newer neighbours waiting their turn. Louann Onions and Priss shouldn't be so familiar already. It is all wrong. It's not the natural order of things.

But the Scuzzies are well and truly back. Watch out for that sinking feeling. Carrie thinks she must be well and truly drowned now. She's never thought of the Scuzzbags with proper names and the fact that their names are so ill-suited is further justification for continued use of their assumed monikers. But knowledge of their surnames did provide her with this plan. She thought about ringing them. It beat going round in person. She planned to phone them up and if they objected to her phoning them out of the blue she would say, 'why, do you find this intrusive?' Then she would go on to tell them how their noise was intrusive and had been for the last few months.

But, neither of them were registered in the phone directory.

*

Day Nineteen

We went to my parents at the weekend. As Sandy and I were walking down the passageway to pick up the taxi we found it peppered with dog crap. Great meaty sausages. But at least the Onions' in Number 5 will have seen and smelt it too—it affects them most of all, having to share that passage with the Scuzzbags.

But I had a dream last night, Mr Vowells. A dream that only a curtain separated our house from next door— the houses were open plan, no party walls. This is what it's come to, Mr Vowells, invading even my dreams. Then the sound of their smoke alarm going off at some unearthly hour intruded my sleep, and so I wasn't even at liberty to dream my boundary-anxiety dreams. This isn't the first time we've heard their alarm. It keeps bleeping and they never get it fixed. It was so distinct I thought it might be ours. But it wasn't ours. I sat on the loo in the dark with the door open, the green light from our smoke alarm shining down like some pole star. I thought that maybe they are putting themselves or us at risk of a fire. Mr Vowells, you have to save me—save us—from this hell. From these dog shit wars. From these boundary disputes. From this rape of our peace. We're counting on you. If I send this off soon, you will be able to read it in one go and get a feel for the development of these problems.

You may think this is small fry compared with what is going on in the wider world, with some countries intent on demolishing others all because of religious or cultural or ethnic differences and how it's a real threat to world peace, especially due to the expansion of nuclear capability, but wars begin small—Sandy is right about that—and we need our own United Nations right here at Pennycott. I suppose nuclear capability for peaceful purposes or war can be looked at thus: if I said to you I was stocking up on petrol for my paraffin stove—you might think it for domestic purposes in peaceful circumstances—but if I talked about setting fire to my neighbours' property, you might view it a bit differently and deny me petrol, but though I do feel like petrol-bombing my neighbours and wiping them off the face of Pennycott, it's one thing to say it, quite another to do it. It's playing a game. I've got weapons in my pocket, you say, like Saddam. But Sandy and I are peaceful people when all's said and done.

*

Sick of the sight of the dog fouling on next door's patio, Carrie decides to phone Chris Vowells' department one Tuesday. Chris Vowells' underling takes the call, assuring Carrie that someone will be investigating. Carrie tells the underling that he mustn't warn the neighbours in advance of their visit, otherwise the neighbours will clean it up. The underling says, 'But that's what you want, isn't it?' Carrie thinks, Hullo? Neighbours will direct a half-hearted hosepipe at it for a few days, then it'll be *back*? She imagines herself speaking in the 'upswing' so maligned by those Grumpy Old Men a few years back. Sandy agreed with the GOM about the upswing, being a GOM himself, and she did feel the same too at the time, which probably made her a Grumpy Old Woman. But now, in secret, she thinks the upswing has a certain power about it. Maybe the underling has picked up the silent vibrations of the upswing because he ends the conversation by agreeing to do some spot checks the following week.

But, ahead of 'the following week', after weeks of neglect, the yard is treated to a thorough hose down, somewhat discrediting Carrie's grievance. Or maybe they've been warned. Maybe that is it.

The knockings and scrapings, after a short reprieve, also begin to creep up again. Carrie thinks how intermittent noise is a huge stressor. It's what torturers use, Clo says, so their victims are always on edge because they never know when the noise will occur, just that it will. Sofe has also spoken to a solicitor about her own noise problem and her solicitor said that noise is a strange thing—that one single loud explosion will be recorded in the highest decibels on all the machines, but it is the quieter relentlessness of everyday noise nuisance that drives people mad. This is an empowering piece of information, especially coming from a solicitor.

On the doorstep, meanwhile, a new slimline telephone directory is waiting for Carrie to strike gold when she looks under the surname Steer.

'So it's *her* name listed, Sandy, look. The bossy mare! No wonder I couldn't find it. I was looking under Woodcock, you know, his name, after the newspaper article.'

'Hmm. You're not going to phone them, are you?'

'Why ever not?'

'It's just that it's quiet at the minute.'

'OK. But just let them dare to make any more noise and I will be on that blower, I swear.'

Carrie doesn't have to wait very long. A little over one hour later, and there are terrible thumps coming from the other side of the wall. She can't hear any screams or rows so she's no idea what it is. Maybe it is the Scuzzy girl and her brat, jumping. She thought being armed with the Scuzzbags' phone number would be empowering but now it fazes her. What was she thinking of? Phones half scare her to death.

She shakes when she picks up the receiver. It feels like a powerful weapon in her hand. She dials 141 before dialling the Scuzzbags' number so that the caller cannot be identified—then her OCD makes her disbelieve she has really dialled 141 and she gets caught in a loop for a while. Then when she finally dials all the numbers—the 141 plus the Scuzzies' number—she hangs up at the first whiff of the girl's mock-respectable telephone voice. The Scuzzy girl will think it's just cold-calling (if she thinks at all). Carrie and Sandy have had a lot of this lately, random dialling from international companies, then a deadly silence on answering before the disconnection or automated recording.

Carrie starts phoning the Scuzzies at unsocial times—first thing or last thing (in the manner of the cold-callers) so they'll know what intrusion feels like. She should go round and speak to them. But the Scuzzies are angry people. If they were easygoing folk like the Zamoras, she could speak to them. Sandy says: 'But you were annoyed with the Zamoras' high jinx, now you're annoyed with the rows. Make up your mind which you want—happy people or angry people?'

She screams at him. 'Why does there have to be only two choices?'

Why isn't he onside any more?

The word onside makes her think of her beloved Liverpool Football Club and calms her down, momentarily. Getting caught up in the weekly dramas is all that matters for those ninety minutes, whether she's watching on TV or listening to 5 Live. Sandy is a neutral, though he has a soft spot for various clubs, including Blue Mooners Manchester City (maybe just because brother Ken is a Manchester United fan) and West Bromwich Albion. But when it comes to strategy and playing positions and X was great playing in a wide right position, Sandy is your man. He is Premier League. He is like those people who phone up on 6-0-6 and have opinions. Who know statistics going back years. He can debate for hours about goalies—who is a fist man, who is a palm man. He can hold his own in a pub (and they have watched matches on the big screen in the pub where you have to sacrifice quality of picture for size). They went to the pub to see Liverpool's historic comeback at Istanbul, seven years ago, enduring some boneheads who weren't Liverpool fans but had turned up anyway to cheer on the last remaining English side in the competition, though jeer on would be a more accurate description of how they gave account of themselves that night. Carrie is not so gracious to Man U fans, whereas when his team's knocked out of the Champion's League or the Europa, Ken supports other English clubs left in the competition—even his deadly rivals. Carrie's not reached that level of magnanimity yet. Sandy may be the strategist, the stats expert, but Carrie is building up her own knowledge-base, her own observations of temperament. Of managers, what they wear. Which come booted and suited, or in track suit and club crest, or in great coat. She knows all their animated hand gestures from the touchline, she knows all the expressions from the commentators. *Oh good save!*

And wasn't the great comeback at Istanbul also the year that Antony Gormley brought his Iron Men to Crosby beach, putting her home town on the map? The beach where she has dim memories of sand-covered clumps of oil, dropped off by passing tankers.

Sometimes she longs to be back in the edgy north and a nineteen-seventies Anfield where her dad took her twice—once in the stands where she was like a kid in the front row of the theatre, her favourite players so large and unreal in the flesh—and once in the Kop. The things she was able to do in those days. She's seen this workshop being advertized in this cranky little south west town— *Rediscover the Northerner in you.* She'd like to. But not at £50 a pop, thanks very much, and certainly not with Mr Hug-A-Tree, the workshop organizer who hales from Yorkshire it is alleged but sounds more Barnstaple than Barnsley.

Carrie is brought back by the sight of Sandy struggling into his jacket.

'Now where are you off to?'

'Number 8. I need some of the old ganja leaf.'

'Well don't hurry back on my account.' Carrie hopes there is the right measure of sarcasm in her tone: just a dash, but not too little to pass him by entirely. These days Sandy seems to stay a bit too long at Fiona's, the hug-a-tree mother of Eden. What's more, Fiona has recently separated from Mr Hug-A-Tree—he of dubious northern heritage. Carrie likes to think Sandy wouldn't, that he's not the sort, where would he find the energy anyway? But all this, this intrusion, this stress, it is getting to him, getting to them both, creating cracks.

A couple of days later, a letter arrives from Mike Naylor, the Housing Resources & Development Manager, full of what Carrie sees as yet more blah. Her blood is hotter than soup as she reads it. All they ever get are Clever Trevors and Trendy Wendys. Not even that clever when she comes to think of it. In fact, pretty obtuse now she reads it again.

First off, it's that loaded word 'allegation', with all its insinuations. *Your allegation of noise nuisance.* Like Mr Naylor doesn't believe it to be the truth. Just like that time she appealed against a Social Security decision and they referred to her 'alleged' problem. The insertion of that word 'alleged' before the word 'problem' made it look like it was all in her head.

Second off, there's that little line *any noise from your neighbour is not thought to be excessive or unreasonable but everyday noise one would expect in such a situation.* Like they don't know there's been a change of neighbours since that initial investigation. Like any future neighbour can never be excessive or unreasonable, amen.

But here comes the mother of all lines: *The Housing Department will address problems of noise if it thought that this constitutes a nuisance and a tenant is considered to be in breach of their tenancy agreement. The advice received to date indicates that this is not the case which is why further action has been limited.*

She sets to work immediately on a reply, without Sandy's input.

Fragments of what'll form part of the finished product start to take shape. *In your previous letter you said "I can assure you we take any anti-social behaviour very seriously and would be grateful if you would inform us of any problems that you may experience in the future" which we did.* Good to quote their own empty words back at them. *With respect, we live here and you don't and we've lived here long enough to know when noise is reasonable and when it is excessive.* It's good to keep the vernacular polite with that little touch 'with respect'. *Also, the repercussions of the first family's placement were felt for months afterwards by the local community and it was generally agreed that this kind of behaviour is* not *"what one would expect in such a situation" but was thought to be excessive and unreasonable.* That deals with that point. The ending will go something like this: *However as a result of your last letter we have now lost faith in your willingness to take our complaints seriously.* She will get some input from Sofe who'll have some more ideas based on her own neighbour disputes. She needs to talk about legal advice. Mention a solicitor. Yeah, that'll put the wind up them. She reads back over her half-formed jottings and rests on her choice of the word 'we'. She and Sandy don't feel much like a 'we' any more. She doesn't even know if they are still in agreement on this matter. He's started to call her a glass-half-empty person, preferring to chat to Fiona Hug-a-Tree who he obviously sees as a glass half full.

The threes are back.

Every day, Carrie plays *Tell Mee, Daphne* three times.

Things seem quieter on the dog front—the younger, noisier Pepper having been dispatched, it seems, to somewhere more suited to his exuberant temperament, while his canine pal completes his cage rest. But now the little sod of a toddler has filled the vacancy left by Pepper. Carrie is subjected to his pounding footsteps, back and forth, forth and back, and his squealing accompaniment, sometimes at midnight. She does a great line in imitations, padding her feet heavily on the spot in bouts of three until it stops. Of course, it's not his fault, it's *theirs*, for not telling him to stop. Mr Vowells and Mike Naylor would describe the intermittent feet as everyday noise, even though it's more disturbing than a regular bass beat. She wishes feet could be impounded like a hi-fi.

Sandy says, 'For Pity's Sake, Carrie! You have to cut people some slack.' He is trying to watch the news when he says this. But the news is stressing her too.

'Touch wood, Sandy,' she screams, at the mention of bombs and terrorist attacks. This touching of wood is back in a big way too, along with the threes. It's no good Sandy just kicking the table with his shod foot, either, it has to be bare flesh, otherwise it doesn't count. Just to make sure, she takes hold of his hand and squashes it against the coffee table, thrice, so she can *know* that his skin has made contact with the wood, not just his nail or his sleeve.

'It's not real wood anyway,' he says, so she brings over his rosewood walking stick, and stuffs the crook in his hand.

'I think you're having one of your episodes again, Carrie.'

She ignores this remark and says she saw the Onions' talking to the Scuzzies earlier. 'They're all conspiring. I thought better of the Onions. I thought they might have joined forces with us, against the Scuzzies.'

The Onions' could have given important substantiation to their case if they, too, had written to the council.

'Cut. Them. Some. Slack.' The rubber bottom of Sandy's stick is used to emphasize each word. Four bangs. Maybe he's into fours. She tells him not to bang his stick loudly because then he'll be giving the neighbours the green light to do likewise.

He pounds his stick even more in defiance—'I can't live like this any more, Carrie. I can't live in a cage'—marking what she fears might be the final u-bend in their relationship. He hoists himself up, puts on his jacket.

'Where are you going? Off to see Fiona?' she shouts after him.

He slams the door behind him.

*

Day Twenty

We have a date for the TV programme, the one Priss contacted about our neighbour problems. That date is in the New Year. January 9th on Channel 5 at 9 pm. A date for your diary, Mr Vowells, because that'll be further evidence of what we've had to go through.

I am Seroxat Man. Seroxat Sid. Seroxat Sid sounds more funky than Seroxat Sue. I've thought all this before. Seroxat Sue sounds too much like a neurotic whinger who needs to get out more. This is bad news for women. There comes a point when you become saturated with Bad News.

I have to touch wood with my bare toe every time death is mentioned on the Bad News (I hate even writing the D word). I have to think bless bless bless all the time, bless my friends and family and loved ones, lest a curse should creep in between the blesses. They can creep in, even if you don't want them to, especially if you don't want them to. You have to tell them go fuck themselves. Pardon the language but you don't mince words when those cusses are about.

It's too cold to have bare toes anyway. But there comes a point when you become saturated with bad news. Did I already say that? I'm not gaga, never worry on that score. Remember 2001? There was a lot of bad news in that year. In September, before the terrorist attacks on the World Trade Centre, the item dominating the news was the Catholic children of Holy Cross who had to run the gauntlet in Ardougne on their way to school. Frightened little five-year-olds. Not a lot of people remember that but I do. News can be a thread that's cut off if something else pushes its way in. It's like a person barging to the front of the queue, only it's a news item with no manners. You can't stick an ASBO on a news item though, can you? But the World Trade Centre came in and the little child looked up at the plane trails in the sky on September 12th and 13th and said to his dad, 'Are they going to burst into flames at the other end?' Then it was we who crossed into Moslem skies. The Taliban were big news in that year, too. You may remember the Ministry of Virtue & Vice and there was no football played in the stadium, just blood on the pitch beneath your blue veil, no balls bouncing off goal posts, no headers, just your neck, mister, swinging and broken, maybe you liked boys or paid for sex or screwed someone else's woman or taught girls under twelve, who knows, but the screaming wasn't to cheer on your national football team, but your public execution. (I expect you're thinking, tell us news not history).

But, I've got the A4 manila envelope ready, all addressed, and tonight I will pop in the journal, and tomorrow I'll take it down to the Post Office to be weighed and send it to you, Mr Vowells. Sorry it's months late, but I will include a covering letter explaining all.

*

The following day, true to her word, Carrie sends off the journal at the same time as sending off her ESA form to the DWP.

A weight has been lifted. Two weights, in fact. They are out there now. In the laps of the sods.

Sandy says she should have let him look at the journal first. He says the council may have her down as a compulsive complainer.

She hears clanging noises next door. Sandy says it was nothing, the noise. He says if they dropped a feather next door, she would be annoyed. She says is it surprising? When the dog hears the bell, it salivates. When she hears them come in, she gets wound up. She's expecting noise now, even if it doesn't come. It's called Classical Conditioning. She remembers that much from her A Level Psychology.

She'd like to know who rattled Sandy's cage, anyway, and how come he got out of bed the wrong side, and before her. When he gets up before her, he leaves her behind. Like he's overtaken her without signalling. She is always left behind now, he has done everything before her—first school, first love, first job, first home. He will even die before her, probably. Leaving her all alone. (She hastily touches wood three times, whispering 'bless bless bless' as she does so. She didn't mean to think of his death). But she never expected Sandy to leave her behind. But he gets up before her and leaves her behind. He gets up before her because he sleeps reasonably. She envies the speed with which he falls asleep. She hears him snoring in the spare room while she lies awake, waiting for noise. There's no point sleeping, if you're only going to be dragged from it. Sandy doesn't worry about sleep like she does. But people kill for sleep, she thinks, remembering a story on the news of a poor old woman sleeping rough who was stabbed to death by a young man, just because he couldn't sleep for her snoring.

Carrie looks at Sandy now with a scrutinizing eye. He seems unfazed by their Situation. Maybe he has an unshakable faith that it'll all come good in the end. Sometimes she looks at him and he looks funny. Not funny ha-ha, but funny different. Like when you break a word down into its components, its individual letters, and the more you think about it, the more difficult it is to know if you've spelt it right. So it is with Sandy. Is it his eyes? No longer big, blue and innocent? Or his whole face, always turned away from her, never meeting her gaze? His speech? Saying one thing but leaking another? She can't read him any more. He's like those people you see on videophone on the news, their movements jerky, their sound not quite matching up. It's like Sandy, too, is far off in a foreign land.

Then he says it.

'I can't do this any more, Carrie.'

She doesn't want him to say any more. She wants to clap her hand across his mouth so nothing more escapes it.

'Christmas will be here soon,' she says. As if

somehow that will save them, will make it all okay.

'Exactly. I need some space. I've spoken to Ken and Dot—'

'Not to Fiona then?'

He shakes his head. 'I'm not even going to dignify that with an answer.'

'You spoke to Ken and Dot? When?' He is another one who's been plotting things, somehow. She took her *eye off the ball*. She laughs inside herself, at how there's always a football phrase to be had.

'I need some space, Carrie. From all this.' He waves his stick around in a semi-circle in the vague direction of the party wall between their house and Number 4. But they both know he means more when he refers to 'all this'.

'You need some space from me. That's it, isn't it?' She feels herself bordering on that angry hilarity as she stands red-faced over him, a concealed tremble about to break in her voice. 'But it's not my fault.' Tears burn down her face. 'You're letting them win.'

He shakes his head, stands up. 'You need some space too. From this. It's tearing us apart, can't you see that?' He squeezes her shoulders. 'I've not got the energy for it any more. It's putting strain on our health. On us.'

'Please don't leave me here on my own...I don't think—'

He sighs. 'Go and stay with your folks for Christmas, or even before, and I'll go and stay with Ken and Dot. But I can't hang on for Christmas.' His hands drop from her shoulders. 'I need to be away from here *now*. I need to recharge. We can review where we're at in the new year. But right now—right *here*—I can't think, Carrie. I can't be myself.'

This is what outside stresses do. They put strain on

relationships, stop you focussing and nurturing the people you care about. They cause fractures. Sandy's right, she's not been able to see how broken he is. She wants him as her rock but that rock's been crumbling. Deep down, she understands. She doesn't want the cracks and fissures to be beyond repair. She wants to see him when all this has gone, when—if she survives it—they can concentrate on their relationship again, nurture it. But how will she deal with all this alone?

'You won't be alone,' he reassures her as he prepares to leave. 'I'll be on the end of a phone or an email or the dreaded Facebook. You've got Sofe just round the corner and Clo a short taxi ride away.' She gives an unconvincing nod as she helps him load his bike into the back of a taxi. She doesn't blame him for wanting some time out. They are both hollowed out. 'And you can always escape to your parents if it gets too much.' She nods again. 'Promise me, Carrie.' They hug. She promises.

With Sandy out of the picture, Carrie reflects on how to get herself to Christmas with her sanity still intact, if indeed, there's any sanity left in the stores. There should be plenty to occupy herself in the run up to Christmas, if only Christmas shopping and shoppers didn't stress her. The more stressed she is, the more she needs to stay at home, but home is no longer a sanctuary. If she could just make it as far as Christmas…because it is too early to land on her folks. What if she should be summoned for a Work Capability Assessment and she isn't there to respond?

Now that Sandy's away, Carrie crashes about in her house, turns her music and TV up full whack. She's sick of observing the rules, of being a prisoner in her own home, where does it get you? She shouts at the music she puts on herself. She decides the best place to find refuge is at Sofe's around the corner. But Sofe has a new man in her life. There's nothing about Sofe's behaviour that isn't welcoming or understanding but it's hard to be around Sofe in her situation — in new-man's-land, where everything is fresh and exciting — when Carrie is in no-man's-land: a place so painfully opposite to Sofe's, her own relationship in tatters.

But at least Clo is free and single, and there for Carrie. This makes Carrie feel a greater affiliation for her at this time. This is what happens when you are a threesome: small shifts in circumstances, a wrong word here, a kind gesture there, and the dynamic subtly changes. Their three-way friendship is organic and fluid as a result, it is strong enough to weather the ups and downs.

Carrie walks as far as the taxi rank most days and takes a cab to Clo's council flat, not returning until under cover of darkness when she feels safer and more hidden. Once back home the noise next door has usually settled and she has Sandy's messages to look forward to.

'We can go to the Christmas market together if you like,' Clo suggests. 'If we can put up with the crowds.'

'I will if you will.' Carrie smiles. She knows Clo is just as apprehensive as she is but the fact that they are both feeling this way gives each a strange sense of daring. Each can help the other and there'll be no recriminations if the other has to pass up on the day.

It's a typical December evening—crisp and frosty—when they venture out in the early evening for the Christmas market. The stalls, having been erected all day, now look bright and festive with candles and fairy lights. Children crowd around the rainbow glowsticks, traditional wassailing songs are being sung under the Butterwalk and polystyrene cups of mulled wine are being sold for £3 a pop. They treat themselves to a cup and it warms the pair of them as they fondle items from various stalls under canvas: a felt pixie hat, should we get this for Sofe, (giggles), a Christmas chutney, oh my mum might like this, she loves figs, and look at these blown-glass baubles and wooden star mobiles!

'Oh, I must have a crêpe,' Clo announces suddenly, recognising the stallholder, someone who seems to be more than an acquaintance, but not quite a friend. 'Mmm, they look lovely, Yaz,' says Clo, huddling up to the warm of the stall. 'I'll have one of your savoury ones—with the goat's cheese and sun-dried tomatoes and basil.' It seems from their following exchange, which Carrie isn't really paying attention to, that Clo knows Yaz through some pilates class.

'This is my friend Carrie. You gonna have one too? I don't want to pig out on my own!'

'Lemon and sugar for me every time.'

'I'm paying,' Clo insists.

Yaz smiles as she ladles some more batter onto the second griddle, which sizzles as she smooths it round with a T-shaped implement, while the other stallholder is busy flipping Clo's crêpe with a palette knife on the first griddle. It is intriguing to watch the art of it.

'Do you live locally too, Carrie?' Yaz keeps her eyes on the crêpe as it sizzles, waiting for the optimal time to flip it, ready for the filling.

'Yes, I live at Pennycott, top of town.'

Yaz runs her palette knife under the crêpe, turning it over on the griddle, before drizzling it with lemon sauce and sugar.

'Pennycott? I think that's where my ex neighbour moved to. Big woman, blond.'

Carrie's mind is blank for a second. Clo has paid for both crêpes and hers is now in her hands, ready to guzzle.

Carrie's own crêpe is being flattened into a cone, before being transferred to a folded-over paper plate and handed to her. 'You mean Priss?'

'That's her.' Yaz shakes her head. 'Awful woman. She and her mother persecuted our family…' She nudges the young man at the other griddle. 'Convinced my son here was being radicalized by Islamic extremists, just because he had a bit more facial growth.'

The young man snickers. 'The mother, she was the worst. Convinced none of us were working because we were sometimes about in the daytime.'

Clo is busy tackling her crêpe, trying not to burn her lips or to prevent the contents from escaping.

Yaz is shaking her head as she oils down her griddle. 'That time when she had that massive row with us over that barbecue for Sami's birthday and the young ones were running around having fun as kids do, remember?'

The young man tuts. 'The music was very quiet and we told most neighbours it was a one-off.'

The sinking feeling is happening somewhere inside Carrie. But there is also a rising feeling.

'Yeah,' Yaz agrees. 'Shouting about the smell of curry wafting over her fence, and she didn't even live there, the mother!' Carrie thinks then, it's not just me. This is what the rising feeling is. Knowing that it's not her, not just her.

'Said we were taking houses from the locals, jumping up the housing list and such crap…'

Clo is beckoning and calling Carrie over, having found a space for two on the nearby circular bench, watching some fire-eaters.

'It's been nice meeting you, Yaz…and very enlightening.' Carrie takes a bite of her crêpe, smiling her appreciation of the sweet warm taste in her mouth.

Carrie's father comes to pick her up a few days before Christmas. She had to tell her parents she wished to come over a bit earlier this year as Sandy had already gone to stay with Ken and Dot. This is nothing unusual: Sandy's Christmas arrangements varying year on year to fit around Ken and Dot.

During the run up to Christmas, Carrie loses herself in her parents' lives and surroundings: in their thatched cottage called Sweet Briar Cottage, always festive and cosy at this time of year. Carrie called thatched cottages 'haired houses' when she was little. There may have been one or two in Little Crosby village when she was a child, her mum would remember. This is what probably started her mum dreaming for a cottage in the country, come to think of it.

'You've hardly mentioned Sandy,' her mother says on Christmas Eve as Carrie is hefting some logs in from outside for the wood burning stove.

She knew her mother would sense something amiss. You can't hide emotional stuff from mothers. 'Where do you want these, mum? By the Rayburn?'

Her mum nods, clearing a space at the side. 'They're very sodden, because of all the rain. When they're dry we can take them through to the sitting room, ready for putting on the fire.'

Carrie's dad intervenes. 'I'll do that,' and shoos Carrie and her mother through to the sitting room. 'You two go and decorate the tree!'

Carrie's mum is waiting anxiously for a reply to her question. 'Is everything all right, Carrie? With you and Sandy? Is he coming over on Boxing Day as usual?'

Carrie sighs, shakes her head. 'We're spending it apart this year.'

'Oh no, darling. Is it his brother? Or his MS? Is it worse?'

Carrie seizes on a mouse. Not literally but as a topic-changer. 'Ooo, did you see him, mum? He shot behind that stack of logs.'

'This cottage is riddled with mice,' her mum says, taking the bait. 'There's one clever little bugger who never gets caught, maybe that's him!' Her mum giggles. 'Or perhaps it's a whole family. Lord knows I've spent out on new Swedish traps, not to mention bars of chocolate, peanut butter, and chocolate spread. The clever little bugger has devoured them all right, but can I catch the little demon?'

'You need a cat.' Carrie hopes that the subject of her and Sandy is suitably buried. *Good save.* She knows her mum won't push it and she welcomes that. She even welcomes the mice. Somehow they bypass her OCD, even though logic says they shouldn't. But there are always different creatures to ponder here. On a visit last spring, she counted fifteen frogs in the pond at one time, plus a dead bird, which her mother scooped out with a spade and buried. Sometimes an alpaca in the adjoining field appears at the fence. It's a funny but increasingly familiar sight in Devon, and they sell socks made of alpaca wool down at the local mill, which is a working mill and has steam-ups on Bank Holidays.

And the only noisy neighbours to be had are up in the eaves. Birds? Mice?

Although Carrie mentions Sandy in passing over Christmas, the subject of their relationship isn't broached again until the night before she's due to leave, in early January, when Carrie's mum pours her an extra large glass of sherry (in spite of her protests—'Steady on, mum, my medication)—and says, 'Are you sure everything's OK with you and Sandy? I do hope you're happy, Carrie. We both do. You're our daughter and you would tell us if anything was wrong, wouldn't you?'

Carrie sips her sherry. 'It's just neighbour trouble again. It's caused us a few arguments, that's all. Nothing for you to fret about.' She finds refuge in a few larger glugs of sherry. 'I'm sure the break has done us both good, away from the situation. In fact, Sandy sounds more chilled, from his Facebook messages.'

Her mum smiles, pats her knee.

Carrie thinks this is true—about Sandy being chilled—though it's hard to gauge. She told him, of course, before Christmas, in a Facebook message, about the chance meeting with Yaz on the crêpe stall and what Yaz said regarding Priss and her prejudices. And those of Priss's mother. It proved that it wasn't all in her head. But Sandy seemed a bit too underwhelmed by the revelation. It will take time, she knows that. Rome not being built in a day and all that. But maybe now Christmas is over, maybe having been away from it all…

Her dad is looking at her with a hearty expression. 'You've put on weight since being with us, luv.' She tries to mask a scowl because he means it is as a good thing, the way fathers do. 'That'll be the Seroxat,' she says. 'I've put on half a stone!' Looks at her mum who says, 'That'll be Christmas!'

New year celebrations over, Carrie braves the train home in a state of fearful apprehension. Never mind the sinking feeling, it is all-out dread. She should have accepted her father's offer of a lift. It doesn't help that Sandy has been vague about the date of his return: possibly today, but maybe tomorrow? After leaving the taxi, she glances over into the garden of Number 4 as she's descending the steps into the passageway, the sense of disquiet alive in her gut, though there's no movement, no changes. Maybe that is it. *No change.* She's coming back to the same as before. This is what the dread will be about, the thought of months and months of more of the same, grinding her and Sandy down—if indeed, she and Sandy are still as one. Through the trellis of Number 4, she sees mounds of dog do still pocking the flags.

Inside the house, she picks up a few late Christmas cards and listens to the new phone messages, including one from Clo to say she's got a nasty chest infection. They have been in touch spasmodically over the festive season on Facebook. There is nothing new from Sandy.

He turns up the following day. Her joy at seeing him not quite reciprocated. Maybe hers isn't joy, but relief. The return of her ally. Her partner in crime. 'Let's just play it by ear,' he says. 'A day at a time.'

On January 9th, Sandy and Carrie are having a rare shopping trip to Morrison's to buy a few essentials. All the while, Carrie keeps her eyes peeled for any sign of Priss on the till, so they can avoid that particular checkout, but then she's distracted by screeching headlines on the front page of the paper they call The Daily Ex-Lax, something along the lines of Labour being the party of shirkers because they voted against freezing benefits to one per cent for three years, along with a handful of Lib Dems who voted against the government. Carrie is almost frothing at the mouth as she turns over a wodge of Expresses and their lying headlines.

'I'm feeling nervous, Sand...to think we're going to be part of the local news tonight.'

He raises his eyebrows quizzically. 'Uh?'

'You *know*. The *programme*.'

'Oh that. I'd forgotten.'

She does one of her smile-frowns. He's kidding. Surely he can't have forgotten.

Whatever the case, at a few minutes to 9 o'clock in the evening, Sandy switches the TV on.

'I feel sick, Sandy.'

'Why? We can record it instead if you like?

She shakes her head. 'No, I'd rather know what's going out live on air.'

She knows it's just nervous apprehension—for this is what she's been waiting for, isn't it? This day of reckoning; when the world will see a window into what their lives have been like and they will be vindicated.

Sandy offers to put the kettle on and while he's making them a pot of tea, Carrie reflects on how they've not heard anything from the Scuzzies since new year, so maybe they've moved out. Maybe she and Sandy won't have to worry about retribution. After all, Priss and the Onions' are on their side, at least as far as the dog fouling is concerned. Or they were, back when this was recorded, weren't they? Carrie cannot remember for certain, so much has gone down since.

The adverts and trailers finish. Sandy lays down the tray with steaming mugs of tea. The programme is announced, immediately followed by clips of neighbourhood disputes. Various residents from around the country and their particular beefs are distilled into headlines. First off, there is some elderly couple in rural Hertfordshire, recounting some boundary dispute involving a stone wall being removed and replaced with high ugly fencing, before cutting to another scene which they don't immediately recognise as Pennycott until they see a close-up of Priss talking. And Priss's mother saying. 'They're just taking the piss, basically.' And Louann Onions saying 'she's nothing but a bully.' Carrie tries to process this, she didn't know all this about the Scuzzies, but then maybe this is why Priss and the Onions have looked conspiratorial on occasion—they've needed to bond against the common enemy. Carrie only wishes she could have been part of their circle.

Then the programme switches to another resident in Scotland, describing some argument about loud music and a personal hate campaign: one set of neighbours fearing for their lives, the other set of neighbours having declined to take part except via excerpts from their solicitor's letters. It looks like being one of those programmes where the format is to keep hopping from story to story as is de rigueur these days.

Carrie clutches Sandy's arm while the Hertfordshire couple regale some of their story, then proceeds to pull out some of her hairs while waiting. They call it trichotillomania, this hair-plucking thing. She looked it up on the internet.

'It's a shared boundary,' a rather gentrified woman in a polo neck sweater and a rural backdrop is saying. 'But they didn't ask permission. We came back from my son's and the wall was all gone and that monstrosity—'(camera pans to fence)—'was erected. It's not in keeping with the cottages at all. But he won't take it down.'

The neighbour—a big ruddy-faced man and a pot belly gives a completely different version of events. He sounds more reasonable than he looks. 'They agreed they wanted me to take down their wall because it was collapsing and covered in ivy,' he explains. 'They said the cost of upkeep was becoming prohibitive.'

Carrie believes the man. There's something that doesn't quite ring true about the woman—and her son—when he appears. There seems to be something personal about their dispute; like they've taken exception to their neighbour because he's a townie and has an accent.

This story is interwoven with the one from Glasgow which more closely fits the stereotype of noisy neighbours playing loud music. Carrie loses concentration. Ordinarily she would follow each detail in the story, but she can only concentrate on her restless and racing thoughts and heartbeat.

After an advertisement break, their own dispute is introduced. A few minutes in, and it's clear that the programme-makers have a different agenda, a different version of events to the one Carrie's been occupying for the past few months.

'OMG, Sandy!'

There's no footage of the troublesome Scuzzies at all, except to say 'they declined to take part in this programme'. No shots of the fouled-up yard (somehow in panning over next door's exterior, the camera misses the crucial evidence altogether) and the main thrust of the programme seems to be concerned with the Onions' and Priss's disputes, although a complicated four-way dispute is touched upon. Sandy appears briefly once or twice, talking about the dog fouling and the noise and his MS, but it's obviously been edited and his view doesn't sound at all convincing or forceful; it doesn't make entertaining TV, except when they zoom in on him quoting one of his maxims: *It is easier to love humanity as a whole than to love one's neighbour.* Out of context it sounds flippant and glib.

It soon becomes clear that the programme is biassed in favour of Priss and the Onions', and it's Carrie and Sandy coming across as the perpetrators. Priss is sitting there, looking an even more bloated version of the real thing, saying all this stuff about squawking on a recorder and knockings on the walls and then there's Louann talking about stroppy notes on cars (to which your film crew were a party, she says). 'One time I saw her with her face pressed up against the window of the house next door,' Louann Onions reports. 'That's *very* intimidating. And she was saying something about an axe. She was doing the actions, swinging an axe outside their window…I was worried that it might be a dress rehearsal.' The camera pans to the outside of Number 4 with a reconstruction of Louann just passing as she did on that day. 'Just here, it was.' The camera pans to the place where Louann is pointing and doing the axe actions. Carrie laughs hysterically, clapping her hand over her mouth. It is such nonsense, nobody could ever...but Louann is in her stride. 'Another time, she switched off the electricity supply to their house from here.' Louann is pointing down to the meter cupboards. 'That has to be illegal, surely? If a neighbour is bothering you, then you do the civil thing and go and speak to them. It's always worked for me.' Runs her hand over her tied back hair. 'OK, these neighbours here have their problems and the dog mess *is* horrendous. It does stink. But they, although actually it is *she*—she did exactly the same to the family before. Yes, they had control issues with their kids, but you have to work with your neighbours, you have to cut them some slack.' Then come the words again. In context. 'She's nothing but a bully. She wouldn't have done it to me because I stand up for myself. She picks on the downtrodden and that's despicable in my book.'

Me. She's talking about *me*. Carrie's not sure if she's saying this aloud. She's not sure if she's laughing or crying but she is shaking. She is hot and flushed, and livid. She is a champion of the downtrodden. Didn't she turn the papers over this morning with the shrieking headlines? Doesn't she regale against the increased use of foodbanks and homelessness and sanctions against the disabled? What else is she but a standard-bearer? How dare Louann? And still Louann is blethering on. 'Another time, she swapped her filthy bin with ours. That's not what you do. You report it to the authorities if you've got a problem.'

The camera switches back to Priss who goes on to describe a whole catalogue of incidents, including loud music, blaring TV and shouting. She produces a stack of pages. 'I was advised to keep incident sheets.' The camera then homes in on a notebook, not dissimilar to the one Carrie recently posted off to Mr Vowells. 'I was advised to keep a diary.' Priss's normally piercing eyes well up with what Carrie can only suppose are crocodile tears. 'They don't do any work. She doesn't want a job. She's one of those job snobs, and thinks everyone should have a job they like instead of what they can get.' The camera switches to Priss's mother briefly, squeezing her daughter's shoulders, as she takes over. 'Yes, she's a welfare scrounger, faking her disability while people like Ellie—my granddaughter, who's in a wheelchair with a degenerative muscle disease—has to fight for every last penny. Well, there are things you can do about such people and we intend to.'

The programme switches back again to one of the other participants but Carrie is incandescent. She has seen enough. To think Priss is just on the other side of that plaster and brick, just a few feet away, watching this same travesty, though if she has any sense about her she will be round at her mother's. The Onions' too, very near, yet protected by an extra house and a flight of steps. To think this rubbish is being transmitted through half the TV sets in the region.

Carrie's upturned palms are splayed out in front of her. 'They called me a scrounger, Sand.' They singled her out while exonerating Sandy, maybe because of the visibility of his disability.

She switches the TV off, paces about, pulling out some more of her hair.

'You're getting a bald patch, Carrie. Leave your hair alone.'

She yelps in outrage. 'Is that all you can say? I'll pull it out if I want. It helps me, so there.'

As she plucks, she thinks how hard she's tried to be a good neighbour. Now all the other neighbours will think it is her. Sandy is right. It is easier to love humanity in the round. It is individual people that suck. Especially those just on the other side of your party wall.

'And what did Priss's mother mean about doing things about *such people?*'

'She's just one of the baying mob, Carrie. She's all bluster.'

Carrie can't believe how calm Sandy is about it all, as if he's crossed over to some other place—a place she wants to be but is denied access. Without him she feels cut adrift, alone in her battles.

Every time Sandy's out, Carrie breaks a few more rules. They think she's a neighbour from hell, so she may as well be. One time, she puts some Bizet on, full blast, leaves it on a loop and goes off into town.

Somebody coughed. Somebody walked across the floor. Somebody breathed. She can't be doing with all this noise.

Someone knocks on the door. Someone from the housing association introducing herself as the new Housing Officer for their area. Carrie doesn't catch her name. Or at least it floats in one ear and out the other. From her midriff, the woman lifts a laminated identity card suspended from her neck on a long blue lanyard, complete with mugshot, her (uncaught) name and the Shires Housing Association logo. She's dressed in a smart navy blue suit and is holding a bunch of keys and a clipboard.

Sandy would be out, damn him.

'As I was on site,' the woman says, 'I thought I'd deliver this by hand.'

Carrie eyes the envelope being handed to her with

suspicion. 'What is it?'

'Shall we step inside?'

In spite of herself, Carrie finds herself admitting the woman into her narrow hallway. The woman closes the door behind her. It is awkward, the two of them standing so intimately in the dark and cramped hall.

'Can we go through?' The woman is looking past Carrie to the open door of the lounge. Carrie is wondering why she's getting a bad feeling about this as the woman follows her through. The woman sits herself down on one of the hard-backed wooden dining chairs, secure and confident in herself, even in other people's houses. She is sorting out things on her phone, tapping something in with the back of a pencil, before looking up and launching straight in.

'I expect you know why I'm here.' When Carrie shakes her head the woman regards her suspiciously. 'No? Well, there have been reports of neighbour nuisance and unacceptable behaviour.' The woman's tone is too-confident and brittle, over-compensating for deficiencies in intelligence, Carrie suspects. But if they sound confident, if they power-dress and have noisy shoes, then they are the business. Carrie has met women like this before, they seem to clone them for work in the housing sector and Jobcentres and in the business world at large. They are not paid for their intellect; they are paid for their efficiency, their stridency, for being driven. Most of all, for their excellence in intimidating others—the poor, the vulnerable, those *furthest from the workplace*. 'We have a duty to respond to any complaints of noise and antisocial behaviour.'

'Antisocial behaviour?' Carrie's voice is raised. She laughs scornfully. 'Me? Who's been saying this?'

The woman curves her hair round her ear. Her scent smells expensive and unidentifiable to Carrie who prefers dabs of natural oil. 'I'm afraid I'm not at liberty to dis—' she tries to say before Carrie snaps her off.

'Oh let me guess. The suggestion is laughable. We're the ones who've been the fucking victims in all this so don't give me antisocial behaviour!' As soon as the f bomb escapes her mouth Carrie knows she's lost the woman, who's now rising from the chair, refusing to engage any more. Carrie's voice is cracking, tears of anger spilling out. 'I'm sorry...I didn't mean to swear...it's just been so—'

'The letter spells out what I have already raised with you: reports of noise nuisance and unacceptable behaviour. It reminds you of your tenancy agreement. We take complaints of antisocial behaviour very seriously. If you wish to raise a complaint then you can go through the complaints procedure on our website. We can arrange for mediation in the first instance…'

Carrie shakes her head. 'I raised my complaints with the council because they—the people next door—are council tenants. This is what you all told us to do.' She wonders if the woman saw the TV programme and concludes she must have. Why else is she so cock-a-hoop?

'I suggest you sort things out with your neighbour—or neighbours—in the first instance. As I say, we can assist with mediation. But if you continue to cause upset and distress to your neighbours, this may result in further action.'

As Carrie closes the door on the woman she catches her knocking on Priss's door through the spyhole.

*

Day Zero (again)

News just in—there's been a dreadful mistake, Mr Vowells. I am the perpetratee, not the perpetrator. There's been a terrible mix-up, crossed wires. I am the complainant, not the complainee. You're the only one who can help me now. But this letter from Shires has come to *me*, warning *me* about complaints of noise nuisance and behaviours, which are causing my neighbours alarm and distress. Not even *us*—no, they have separated me from Sandy, they must think he's in the clear. They're not known for their quick reactions at Shires, either. So I hope you will pull your finger out, Mr Vowells. I haven't shown Sandy the letter yet. I should really show him, but he'd be as outraged as me, I'm sure. He would phone Shires, or send it back to them with a clever, covering letter of his own, not curt, but viciously polite, laying the politeness on with a trowel, and who could blame him? It's inexcusable. So inexcusable, in fact, that I don't even want to go there. I shall bin the letter—but the mistake will all be cleared up when you act on the long and detailed logs I sent you.

I am continuing to record my tracks for you, Mr Vowells, until these injustices have been aired and redressed. I know I'm not a perfect citizen, but I do my best. But sometimes, a lot of the time, well, nearly always, I am under great stress and fear of them taking my money away. We're scared. Scared they're going to make us work until we're sixty-nine because of the pensions' crisis. Scared of losing our security. Our social security. Because that's what it used to be called. None of this welfare nonsense. We're scared they're going to make us do too many hours in a week than we can cope with and take our control away from us. They use words like incentivise when what they really mean is sticks, not carrots. Sanctions and cuts. That's all that's happening around us. Snip and slice, and all the shreds are lying like broken debris around us. Strong woven nets of safety that took years to embroider—gone. But they don't take anxiety and stress and depression and OCD and trichothingy seriously. Do the internal organs not count? If I need to keep weeing or crapping or if I get a headache every day or palpitations, aren't these physical? I'm scared, scared of being in my house because of noise. Scared of going out of my house because of coming back to noise. Scared in case I cross a patrolled border. I'm sure you're getting my drift, Mr Vowells. I am scared of a lot of things. At least I am brave enough to admit I'm a coward.

I am only another Seroxat Sid in the eyes of the authorities. Maybe not even that...

I am not mad, I have all my faculties about me, though I don't think Shires think I'm mad anyway, otherwise they wouldn't have issued their warning letters. I know I'm not an exemplary neighbour, but I'm all right. I've tried my hardest. But when you remove the covering of anxiety there is always depression underneath and depression is a terrible thing, Mr Vowells.

It makes you angry. Or you were angry to start with and that gets you down. Then everything starts to get you down. Like seeing those people all loved up with jack shit to worry about but a bit of bad weather, or those with perfect babies and yet still aren't happy, or those at the top of their career, leaping from one success to another. All those with charmed lives. Of course, your bitterness is veiled if the sickening happiness comes from people you know, you have to look or pretend to be happy for them—like I felt with Sofe and her new man—when secretly you're wanting it all to go to hell in a bucket. Sometimes, you can't even pretend, you can't cope with all that Happy Ever After shit and so your successful happy friends become ex-friends. Does that sound horrid? But you can't help it. All those obsessions, the thing with the threes, other people's noise pollution—they get in the way of happiness, I guess.

I had this fella once—years ago, even before Iain who took off to Goa—gave me an old blanket for my birthday. The blanket had a cigarette burn in it. Anyway, this fella said the blanket had a lot of sentimental value, he was very attached to it as it had been camping and round the festivals with him, and so I was pleased with it. *Get me. Pleased.* The dirty cheapskate couldn't even be arsed to buy me a proper present. The blanket was a tatty old thing and wasn't even his to give anyway, it was his landlady's. But that was lack of self-worth, Mr Vowells, that's what. Satisfied that someone should give me a bloody old burnt blanket that wasn't his to give. Because he was a bit hunky and in those days I wanted to marry a face I fancied. Not for me, Soft and Cuddly. Or Bearded and Intellectual. Or Kind and Comical. I wanted Oozing Stud with Knobs on. But we change. We settle for. *That* is depressing.

These things also make me depressed: theme parks, reality TV shows, political correctness, *I see you baby, shaking that ass,* people who are always happy. Life is simply something to get through, like work—or how I imagine work to be. Strip away the gloss and that's what you have. Something to get through. I like events to be over. I've never enjoyed going out, if the truth be known. Even when I used to go out with Iain or the Burnt Blanket, I couldn't wait to get home, put my feet up and review the experience from afar, like watching a film. I like it when a packet of biscuits is finished, so I can chuck the packet away. It's the finishing things with me, not the doing them. That's how I feel about life in general—I'll be relieved when it's all over. Oh I'm not suicidal. I want my allotted time. Going out and happy occasions just stress me. Or depress me. That's all. I don't have the thrill-seeking gene. I have the endurance gene. I saw something about it in a programme once.

And another thing that annoys me—or did do, they don't do it so much now—but it was the thing in soaps at one time, never to show a baby crying. Instead, they played a tape of a baby bawling while the baby's head was turned away from the camera but you could tell the baby wasn't really crying by the movement or angle of its head. Do they think viewers are stupid? It was Political Correctness gone mad. Like it was wrong to show a baby crying, but hullo? Babies *cry*? I don't know why they just didn't put up a disclaimer at the end and have done with it. *No babies were harmed in the making of this programme.*

Sandy agrees with me, or he did do, but we're not agreeing on much else any more. I think we're heading for a split. As in permanent. Our relationship is like elderly skin: sagging, lost its tautness, no edge. 'Look what you've become,' Sandy said recently. 'Dependent, controlling, paranoid.' It was a day or two after the Neighbours' Programme. He shot the words at me like cannon balls. He said I needed a war with the neighbours—both sets—and that I enjoyed it. He said I'd made us unpopular and friendless, that I'm a control freak and that I'd come between his friendship with the O'nions'; that they had a point which they made very publicly and that point was that we're not blameless. He said I should get out more. The soap opera shrinks when you leave the room he said. He's projecting of course. *He's* controlling. *He's* un-neighbourly. *He* needs to get out more. I thought we were united. We stood strong through all the disputes we've had to suffer. Maybe it's

205

the neighbours' fault. They've exposed the cracks in our relationship and stressed us so much that they've driven us apart. You hear about these things happening, don't you? And we did spend Christmas apart. He couldn't take any more.

But I'm not paranoid. People park in my parking space and play their music loud just to annoy me. That is real.

And then there's the council's Big Mistake, Mr Vowells. People like Mike Naylor telling me what is normal everyday noise. I wouldn't profess to know the sights and sounds in his house from not having lived there, so I'd thank him not to tell me about what I hear in mine. If you wouldn't mind passing that on to him, because there's an injunction on my free speech, as good as. But a house is like a body, you know your own best, no one else knows, not even your doctor can know as well as you what's usual and what's unusual. He takes his lead from you. And you only know that from living in it every day. Just like a house. Sofe says I should take it to a solicitor like she's done. Or the ombudsman and get some compo. I said, Sofe, I will take it to the European Courts if I have to because they will know whether it's my right to quiet enjoyment of my home or my neighbour's right to enjoyment of his.

Here's a bonus track from Seroxat Sid, the man with a plan in his head ain't dead. Not yet dead from the smell of the heaps of dog shit still festering over the fence along with the fourteen sacks and the dumped furniture. The rubbish means they've gone. Seroxat Sid says: Good riddance to bad rubbish. Then the man comes from the council, that one who does the electrics, Sid sees his van and goes round next door. *Sid is here, never fear.* The front door is open, Sid waltzes in. Asks him if the garden is going to be cleared and the dopy spark hasn't even seen the garden. Seroxat Sid casts an eye about the kitchen. Looks a state, skirting boards chewed and filthy. The spark says something about the burnt plug upstairs and Sid stomps upstairs for a dekko. You can't stop Seroxat Sid. He sees the burnt socket and the smashed wall in the main bedroom and the broken wardrobe door and the mouldy carpet. Thinks Sid: And didn't your colleague say something about no breach of tenancy? Your colleague say the people they house here are just people who can't afford to buy their homes? Hu*llo?*

And then the next day he sees your men digging a hole in the earth in the corner patch and bury all the months of shit, all ripe for some new kiddies to stumble upon when they're playing or some young mum when she's planting some bulbs...

*

They've gone. Carrie should be feeling jubilant, but she feels surprisingly flat. At one time, she'd have been bursting to tell Sandy about the state of Number 4, about the probable eviction or moonlit flit of the Scuzzies but it's too little too late. Sandy's hardly ever in residence. He comes and goes, collecting things here and there, sounding evasive, returning late at night and sleeping over in the spare room, if he returns at all. She sometimes sees him pass her window in his peaked cap with Fiona Hug-A-Tree and her daughter Eden. He looks relaxed with them, lighter somehow. Fiona with that permanent but impersonal smile, that beatific but tide-out expression in her eyes, where everyone is wonderful but the individual is easily forgotten and not registered.

Carrie says to him one evening when he returns at teatime, 'Why don't you move in with her?'

He flumps his jacket at his feet, rests his stick—the spotted one—between them on the settee. He blows his breath out which has curry-spiced hummus on the end of it. Clearly he's partaken in one of Fiona's sickeningly healthy lunches.

'I'm not having a relationship with Fiona, if that's what you're worried about.' Carrie screws up her eyes, as if this will block any more words. It would be better if he were. 'We're just friends.' So he prefers Fiona's friendship to her own. This is the ultimate betrayal. 'And Eden is a smart kid, it's good to be around that sort of energy.'

Oh god. Her *energy*. He's even sounding like Ms Hug-A-Tree now.

'Don't tell me…Fiona understands you and listens to you.' She lifts his stick slightly and starts poking at his jacket, as if stoking a fire. She imagines him having to take his shoes off each time he enters the Hug-A-Tree household and struggling with it because of his MS. Isn't that part of the etiquette chez the Hug-A-Trees? Or have the rules been relaxed since the departure of Mr Hug-A-Tree? She imagines Fiona cutting Sandy's toenails for him, this intimate thing that only she has been allowed to do. It feels worse than the thought of them sleeping together. The poignancy of it pricks her eyes. She stops prodding his jacket and slides his stick towards him. 'Well, don't stay here on my account or because you think the house situation is too complicated for you to leave.'

He shakes his head, rubbing the settee arm with his middle finger. 'No, no. I wouldn't do that to you. Let's just see how things pan out, eh?'

'They've gone,' she says at last. She'd been looking forward to saying this for so long and now it feels futile. 'Next door have gone. I saw all the damage to the skirtings where the dogs had clawed and a smashed-out hole in their bedroom upstairs. That will have been the time they had that almighty mother of all rows, do you remember, when Paddy got out and was run over? And there was a burnt socket…we used to hear their alarm going off…' She wipes the heels of her hands over the tears, now in free fall, her mouth puckering in unison. 'But it's too late. I've been vindicated and it's too late. For us.'

He lifts a thumb to a fresh tear. 'Shhh now, Carrie.' Then he reaches across and hugs her. She's so missed being wrapped in his 15 tog embrace. 'Shh, it's OK, it's OK. That's good news, eh? Bit of peace for a while.'

She snorts a snotty laugh. 'Yeah until the next lot of losers move in.'

He laughs. 'That's the spirit.' He looks over at the storage space below the television. 'How about a DVD after the meal? There's *The Life Of Pi* which we've still not watched?'

Sandy is away at Ken and Dot's when the letter comes (though Carrie prefers it when he is staying with them, rather than at Fiona's—Ken and Dot at least have their best interests and their relationship at heart.)

She hears the decisive metal flap of the letterbox and immediately gets the sinking feeling. The drowning feeling. She puts off the inevitable, turning over under her duvet, willing for more sleep to come, but it doesn't. She moves in a gingerly fashion from her bed, from her room, to the banister rail. She clocks the unwanted fat tongue of letters poking into her private space. Even up here, she can see one of them is the right brown, the *wrong* brown, amid the sandwich of junk mail.

She stands at the top of the stairs, rigid with dread. If only there was a rewind button or better still, an erase one. A parallel version of this universe where there is no brown envelope. Perhaps it is nothing. Perhaps it's something else, maybe from the council about her housing benefit and council tax, although this isn't the time of year for them to be writing. In a flurry of determination, she descends the stairs and makes a grab for the clump, tossing the fat white junk ones aside and seizing upon the brown offender. She snorts. 'D W fucking P. Department of Worthless Pricks. How did I know?' She tears it open, half expecting and half hoping it's a decision regarding her ESA, whether it has been awarded, whether she will be called for an assessment. Instead she opens up the folded sheet of paper:

Dear Miss Cornish

We are updating your details and need to see you to review the information we currently hold on your claim. There may have been changes that you have not yet told us about. It is important that you attend, if you do not it may affect your benefit.

To avoid unnecessary delay, please bring this letter with you and show it to reception immediately on your arrival. Please ask for Tracey Head.

Please arrive promptly, as it will be difficult to fit in another appointment if you arrive late. If you cannot keep this appointment contact me immediately on the direct number above to arrange another time.

Things that I will need to see:
Proof of identification, such as:

passport

*driving licence
utility bills
rent agreement
bank statement*

Evidence to support your claim to benefit ~~as follows~~*:*

yours sincerely

Tracey Head
COMPLIANCE OFFICER

Something goes off in her. So that thinking to call Sandy or Clo or Sofe doesn't penetrate the steam and red mist. There's nobody here to keep her in check. It's that word Compliance Officer. It's the straw that breaks…It's that sentence *There may have been changes that you have not yet told us about.* She's all too aware of what it means. Someone has reported her for fraud. She strides outside in her dressing-gown, the letter still shaking in her hand as she raps on Priss's door with the other.

'Come on, somebody answer it, I know you're in there!' She marches her way round to the back gate, a tall wooden one like hers, that catches on the concrete above the flight of steps. She forces it open and sees Priss's mother standing near the open back doorway.

From her elevated position at the top of the steps she should feel more powerful, but the dressing gown only makes her feel more vulnerable.

'I know it was you, you malicious old—'

'Oi!' The grond woman's lips are pursing and her neck jutting forward so that all the taut sinews are enhanced. 'If you don't leave I will get straight on to Shires about you harassing me in my own back garden.'

'Do what you like. You can't take any more away

from me, you narrow-minded brainless—'

The woman advances on Carrie, bearing a soggy muddy trowel in her hand. 'Keep away from me, you parasite on the state. You're nothing but a sponger.' She looks as enraged as Carrie feels. 'My granddaughter is going through hell trying to get her benefits because of people like—'

Shut up, shut up, Carrie wants the stupid brainwashed sniping to shut up. This is what those right-wing daily rags do to the unintelligent, they fill their unquestioning heads with propaganda and venom and bile, which they spout without critical thought or question. The garden spade, hitherto stuck in the ground, and that somehow finds itself in Carrie's grasp is being held up against Mrs Priss who drops the trowel as she advances and wrestles Carrie for it. She makes a grab for the end of it, refusing to let go, causing Carrie to lose her footing and take an awkward tumble over the steps. There's a violent clonk on her head, courtesy of a stone tub on her way down, before hitting the ground with a blinding flash.

*

Day Break

A woman who sustained a head injury in an argument with her neighbour in the Pennycott area of Dartbridge has regained consciousness. Her condition is still described as critical but stable...

I remember those words. Do I? Did I dream them instead?

I can't remember. I know I'm in the middle of writing something and it begins Day something. But as I am feeling a broken day, that might be what it is. My head throbs. The words have twins, doubles. Sentences are going missing.

My mother is holding my hand which she strokes every so often. My dad is making jokes, I think. When I next open my eyes they are gone. Yes, I know who you are. Sandy. But I can't remember how I came to be here. No, really. Do I remember the police coming, asking me about 'the incident'? What is the last thing I remember? Please, please. Holding my hands to my head which is bandaged. My head hurting.

Maybe it's later when Sandy shows me get well cards from Clo and Sofe—I think I can picture them—and asks if I remember the neighbours. If I screw up my eyes I see a lady called Judith? Living next door? Edith, oh Edith was it? Yes. And the Zamoras on our other side.

Doctors shine things into my eyes and check my temperature and ask me what the date is. Do I remember the police? Yes, police have been here, asking me questions but I'm not sure what it is I'm supposed to have done. My head throbs. I think I have thoughts on repeat. I have a bandage on my head and they tell me I've been here a few days. Or is it a few hours?

Sandy says he will take me home when I'm enough well. He won't leave my side. He whispers to me 'I was hoping we could have tried for Actual Bodily Harm or worse but she's arguing trespass and self-defence, saying it was an accident...and there were no witnesses, so it doesn't look as if there's a case to answer. Not with you as you are.'

I look at him blankly. I have no idea what he's talking about.

He titters. 'Seeing Priss ashamed and grovelling is enough for me, though it's not really her we have a beef with.'

I think Priss may be one of the nurses. All these names of people I feel I should know but my headache is frightful so I'll take a rest now.

Day Care

We wait in the hospital foyer for the driver to take us home. 'He's a volunteer,' Sandy tells me. 'You know, the driver.' I think he's told me this before. He goes over other things for me as my memory is shot to bits apparently. 'Now, as I said, I've sorted out your benefits,' and when I look at him frowning he waves it away. 'We're both to get some help. Me because of my MS and you because of your head injury. Remember?'

I'm nodding uncertainly because I have a feeling I should. Nod. 'I'll do what I can, of course, but they've assessed both our needs. We're to get some domestic help, cleaning, cooking preparations, that sort of thing. It will take the pressure off me at home. The discharge team have arranged for some therapy and treatment for a period.'

They must think I'm well enough to go home. I know what a kettle is and a bath is and how to make a cup of tea. I know my name and address but I am hazy on a whole time period, which is quite worrying when you think about it. Sandy talks about a whole batch of things that leave me disorientated in time and place, like when you can't put your feet on the ground in water. That feeling.

Once home, I am to keep a diary, to help me remember. To remind me if I forget. Sandy says I'm good at keeping diaries. I am. I have old ones dating back to our first dates together. The records that were out then, the music we shared, the places we lived. 'What was in the news,' Sandy says. I smile and nod. 'You mean when Thatcher got deposed? And Tony Blair took over?' Sandy's looking pained. I think I've not quite got it right. 'If you'd kept your other diary,' he says. 'The one you sent off to that Environmental Health chappie, it might have helped you, like a bridge, over the ground that's difficult for you.'

A big woman with blond hair calls with a mini rose for me in a pot. Pale lemon. Sandy takes it from her. 'You can plant it in the garden later in the year,' the woman says.

Sandy is trying to usher her out. 'Carrie is tired now, Priss. So if that will be all?'

'Yes. Sure. I just thought I'd bring it round. Tell Carrie I'm thinking of her and wishing her well.'

Sandy makes a grunt and says 'two-faced cow' on closing the door. 'And no apologies from her bitch of a mother.'

And so the days turn into weeks, with people coming and going in our house. Cleaners, helpers, OTs, even the police. No, I still can't remember the day my head got hurt, I have to tell them. Sandy seems to think I've lost several months. Will they come back? The specialists say that's what we're all working towards, Carrie.

Day Ja Vu

I am here at the hospital for some or other follow up visit. They tell me I'm doing well. People are buzzing around the wide reception area, looking at signposts—for the café, for the toilets. I cling on to Sandy. 'Please let's sit down.' He finds a spare plastic bucket-seat attached to others and indicates for me to sit there, and the person next to me, on seeing Sandy's stick, rises and makes a gesture to his seat. 'Please,' he instructs Sandy. 'Thanks.' Sandy lowers himself next to me.

'I'm feeling dizzy, Sand.' I close my eyes, trying to ward off a full blown panic attack. All these people, all these bright colours, everything moving. 'Take some deep breaths,' he says, his hand on my back, stroking it reassuringly. I am fighting clammy waves of nausea and then I make a beeline for the toilets.

It is crowded in here too but as soon as one is available I bolt into the loo, slide the lock across the door and sit on it, head in hands, shaking, trying to calm my thoughts and put into action some of the therapy of the last few weeks.

I hear my door rattling, like a kid has just bashed into it, there's a voice of a mother scolding it. More clattering, then briefly a little child face—a boy's—looking under my door from the next cubicle before being reprimanded more forcefully by his mother. I sit a while longer before flushing the loo, slipping open the lock and stepping out into the crowded sink and dryer area where a boy is messing around with the water. The boy is playing with his little brother—the one (I think) who looked under my door. 'Bailey, stop that now!' the mother shrieks. 'Logan, if you don't stop this minute I swear you'll feel my hand on your bum.'

Bailey? Logan? But I know these people. What's more I *remember* them. Each of the boys has grown into the next size up in Little Hooligans. I find myself smiling at the mother (I can't remember her name, if I ever knew it) and her hair looks the wrong colour. She smiles back and rolls her eyes about her two boys. There's a look of recognition on her face, we are both freed from the tyranny of living next door to each other. Or maybe she recognises me but can't quite place me. My memories are like those photos where certain key bits are highlighted (I remember they were noisy neighbours) but the rest is blurred and out of focus. We wash our hands almost simultaneously and examine our reflections in the mirror. She gives me another grin as she leaves which I reciprocate, smiling down at the boys.

I can't wait to tell Sandy, but then something holds me back.

Day Return

And so it happens. Bit by bit. Like morning mist gradually burning off as the day wears on, as the sun clears it away. There are still patches of mist and a huge pall of fog over the day when I was supposed to have clonked my head and the days afterwards when I lay unconscious in hospital.

Even when pieces are returned to me, they are often just that, pieces. Like the neighbours with the dogs. I remember those people, but not their names. I know we didn't like them and they were noisy. I reveal this much to Sandy, so he knows there is hope for my condition. Yet Priss and her infernal mother and Fiona up the way have come back to me with startling clarity. Of course I'm not divulging any of this to Sandy. Not ever. Would you if you were me? Neither will I let on to Priss. I feel empowered knowing, while they still think I don't.

Number 4 next door is no longer in the hands of the council. While I was fuzzy and receiving treatment for my head injury, Sandy saw a solicitor who wrote a letter on our behalf to the council. 'If only we'd done that earlier,' Sandy says. I smile at him. 'The house is now in the hands of an agency,' he says.

As for Seroxat Sid he's pulling out his pink punk hair to make gonks with, but prefers twos to threes. He and me are next door neighbours, living side by side in the one skull, peacefully, it can be done. He is my neighbour from heaven, ready to sort things out if they should ever get tough. But mostly he is now my sleeping partner on the other side of the party wall in my brain.

Sandy switches off the TV. 'Can I make you a hot chocolate before bed?'

I beam at him and nod enthusiastically. 'You're a real gem, Sandy. Do you know that?'

'An opal, d'you reckon? Or an emerald maybe?'

And that's all the news for tonight and for this track of my life, our life, because all we want—all we ever wanted—is blissful, much underrated obscurity. Or to put in another way: the quiet life.

So please don't think we're rude, will you, if we pull down the blinds, close the curtains and switch off.

####

Afterword

Much of this novel has been informed by personal experience, directly or indirectly. I have experienced neighbour problems and like Carrie I have always suffered with anxiety and related problems. In addition I now have additional long term physical illness. I have learned that the two are intricately connected: that is, the quality of your home or lack of it can help or hinder your mental and physical health. Even if you don't have mental health problems to start with – I have known fair-minded people be driven bonkers by neighbour noise and behaviour. It is a curious relationship we have with our neighbours, living cheek by jowl, but with a different set of rules when bricks and cement separate us.

Along with countless friends and family, I have also had direct experience with the benefits regime, for regime is the only way to describe it. I have been a keyboard campaigner on social media since 2010, trying to keep abreast with all the changes to empower myself and others. You will find me - along with untold others – protesting and blogging against inequality and the targeting of the most vulnerable by the Department of Work & Pensions and their lackeys.

Since the Welfare Reform Act of 2012, a whole raft of measures has been introduced in the name of austerity, the most cruel of these against the most vulnerable in our society: the long term sick and disabled. The Work Capability Test (WCA) has been harder and harder to pass, Disability Living Allowance (DLA) has been replaced with Personal Independence Payment (PIP) and vulnerable people have lost the immediate right to appeal against a wrong decision, until they go though a

Mandatory Consideration first. Even before Mandatory Reconsideration was introduced, people dropped out before appeal stage. Now with one more hoop to jump through, many more give up. It is all too much for people already vulnerable, stressed, fatigued, in pain. The cynics among us know that fewer people appealing will mean fewer people getting what is their due.

Furthermore, sick and disabled people can have their benefits sanctioned. Sometimes the most vulnerable have been an easy target by Job Centre staff who have sanctioning targets. There has been a sharp rise in those with mental health disabilities being sanctioned, sometimes for over six months or more. Meanwhile, several hundred disabled people are losing their Motability cars and scooters every week and 18-21 year old ones are no longer being routinely paid housing benefit. Since 2017, cuts of £30 a week have been made for new claimants in the Employment & Support Allowance, Work-Related Activity Group (ESA WRAG) from a paltry £100 a week, even though people in the ESA WRAG group have passed one of the most difficult tests in the world to pass - the flawed Work Capability Assessment (WCA). New proposals are being drawn up at the time of writing to coerce the most severely long term sick and disabled, those in the ESA Support Group, into work. Tax Credits for disabled and non-disabled people alike have been slashed, making it impossible for many of those those who can and want to work, especially the self-employed.

Tragically, many of those who have been wrongly declared fit for work or sanctioned have died before ever getting any justice. Some of the more well known names are David Clapson, Karen Sherlock and Mark Wood.

There are many many more.

Since the Welfare Reform Act 2012, Legal Aid for welfare cases (ergo access to justice) has been scrapped, the Independent Living Fund has been cut, the Bedroom Tax has been introduced, and the use of food banks has rocketed for the working and out of work poor. Homelessness has increased and many more children are living in poverty.

The third child 'rape clause' in order to qualify for benefits for that child is perhaps one of the most pernicious of all policies of a government that has lost all sense of humanity.

Universal Credit is supposed to make things simpler and 'make work pay'. It has been dogged by major IT problems since its inception. People on the ground and MPs across the political spectrum called for a pause in its roll out in order to iron out its many problems, especially delays of 6-8 weeks or even longer before claimants get any income and have warned of a '**disaster waiting to happen**' and '**a human and political catastrophe**'. But this has been ignored. And at the time of writing, October 2017, the misery will be intensified due to the national rollout. Rent arrears will mean more evictions and homelessness. Universal Credit will soon be coming to a town near you, if it hasn't already.

In 2016, Ken Loach's outstanding film *I, Daniel Blake* was released. It highlighted many of the tragedies of welfare reform. The film couldn't come soon enough. Those of us on the ground having predicted and witnessed its devastating effects for years.

If you are outside the UK, some of this may sound strikingly familiar. To others, it may seem like something from a dystopian novel.

Kate Jay-R, 2017

Glossary

Agoraphobia

Literally means 'fear of the market place'. Not all agoraphobics are housebound but all will experience extreme fear and panic in public places and the overwhelming need to escape

ASBO

Antisocial Behaviour Order, particularly but not exclusively used against teenagers and young people causing a nuisance or distress in public. The ASBO was abolished and replaced with something similar in 2015

Con Dems

The Coalition of Conservatives and Liberal Democrats forming the UK Government from 2010-2015

DLA

Disability Living Allowance. A disability benefit being phased out and replaced by Personal Independence Payment (see below)

DWP

Department of Work & Pensions, responsible for benefits and pensions in the UK

ESA

Employment & Support Allowance, a benefit paid to people unable to work due to long term ill health or disability

Environmental Health Officer (EHO)

Employed by local authorities to deal with noise and other public health matters

Housing Association

Non-profit organization to provide low cost rented and shared ownership properties for people on low incomes.

Incapacity Benefit

An out-of-work benefit for the long term ill and disabled, subsequently replaced by Employment & Support Allowance

Nigel Farage

Former leader of The UK Independence Party (UKIP) who led the campaign to lead Britain out of Europe

OT

Occupational Therapy or Therapist whose work it is to help rehabilitate disabled people in everyday activities

PIP

Personal Independence Payment, replacing DLA, and usually involving a face-to-face assessment

Radio 1

A BBC radio station in the UK, playing largely pop music

Radio 4

A BBC radio station featuring current affairs and plays

Seroxat

One of the SSRI antidepressants. Generic name is Paroxetine. Branded as Paxil in the United States

Universal Credit

Former DWP Minister Iain Duncan Smith's flagship welfare reform programme designed to roll six benefits into one and make work pay. Dogged with IT problems and highly criticised for long delays in payments, leaving people in rent arrears and a rise in homelessness and use of food banks

WCA

Work Capability Assessment, a highly criticised assessment carried out by private companies on behalf of the DWP to remove as many people from disability benefits as possible. Has repeatedly been declared as 'not fit for purpose' and is feared and despised by sick and disabled people

Printed in Great Britain
by Amazon

49392003R00135